The Crystal Trail

Linda urged Amber forward in the snow. "Where's my brother?" she asked anxiously.

Laurie pointed up the trail. "Trouble," she said. "I think—"

"Listen!" Linda cut her off.

They stared through the curtain of falling snow, hearing hoofbeats but unable to see the horse racing straight for them.

"It must be Bob's horse, Rocket," Linda said hopefully. "But Bob's riding him too fast for this weather!"

Linda rose in her stirrups, trying to make out the horse and rider. With a sick feeling Linda saw that Bob wasn't riding him at all.

Rocket's saddle was empty!

Books in The Linda Craig Adventure series:

Available from MINSTREL Books

THE LINDA CRAIG ADVENTURES™ #4

THE CRYSTAL TRAIL

By Ann Sheldon

A MINSTREL® BOOK

PUBLISHED BY POCKET BOOKS

New York   London   Toronto   Sydney   Tokyo

A MINSTREL PAPERBACK *ORIGINAL*

 A Minstrel Book published by
POCKET BOOKS, a division of Simon & Schuster Inc.
1230 Avenue of the Americas, New York, NY 10020

ISBN: 0-671-64037-2

First Minstrel Books printing November 1988

10 9 8 7 6 5 4 3 2 1

1 ◆◆◆◆

"Look!" Twelve-year-old Linda Craig's dark eyes were wide with excitement as she leaned across the rear seat of the station wagon and pointed out the window. "You can see it from here!"

Her older brother, Bob, stared into the valley far below the twisting Rocky Mountain road. "That must be the place," he agreed.

In the center of the green valley was a big white ranch house, with barns and stables and several log-cabin bunkhouses.

Glancing over from behind the steering wheel, Linda's grandfather Tom "Bronco" Mallory gave an approving shake of his head. "Nice little spread," he said. "Probably was a working ranch before it turned into a riding school. Horse ranch, I'd guess. That grass would make for good grazing." He spoke with a professional's tone—he was a rancher himself.

"Really, dear," Doña Rosalinda Mallory teased her husband. "I think Linda and Bob are more interested in the riding than the grazing."

Bronco laughed. "You're right. I forgot this was a kind of vacation."

It was about time, too, Linda thought. Ever since she and Bob had come to live at Rancho del Sol in southern California, after their parents had died in an accident, she'd never seen Bronco take so much as a day off.

"Next you'll be telling me that driving to Colorado is an adventure," Doña said. "And speaking of adventures, I want you two to take it easy on those trails up into the mountains." Her tone was scolding, but Linda and Bob both knew their grandmother was kidding them. It seemed no matter where they went, adventure followed.

"I'd hate to be around these mountains in winter," Bronco said. "Ice would really make this place live up to its name—Crystal Valley."

Doña broke out laughing. "Trust you to think of that," she said. "I don't think we have to worry about winter setting in just yet. It's late summer, and Linda and Bob will be here for only two weeks."

" 'Two of the most exciting, challenging weeks' of

my life," Linda said with a grin, quoting from the camp's brochure.

"Hey, are you sure you're ready for that?" Bob asked, his blue eyes twinkling. Teasing Linda was one of his favorite things about being an older brother. Linda, however, did *not* believe that three years older meant three times wiser.

The road took them down into the valley and onto a gravel drive. Bronco slowed the car down. "I don't want to throw up any more gravel than necessary," he explained, smiling. "Otherwise, I might frighten the other campers back in the trailer."

Bronco was referring to Linda's palomino mare, Amber, and Bob's bay gelding, Rocket. They were going to the camp, too.

The station wagon and trailer passed through a gate with a wrought-iron sign that said "Crystal Valley Ranch—A Riding Camp." Bronco stopped the car and rolled down his window as a man with a clipboard waved them down.

"I'm Hank Harrington, the camp director," the man introduced himself. "Welcome to Crystal Valley, Mr. . . ."

"Mallory," Bronco told him. "I'm bringing Bob and Linda Craig."

"Right." Hank Harrington checked something off on his clipboard. "This road will lead you to a big circular driveway." He smiled. "You can't miss it—just look for the wall-to-wall horse trailers. One of the counselors will help unload the horses"—his smile got bigger—"and the campers."

Bronco thanked Hank Harrington and started up the drive. The circular driveway *was* hard to miss—it was jammed with other station wagons and pickup trucks. Just as Hank had said, they were all hitched to horse trailers. Bronco pulled up at the end of a line that extended out onto the gravel drive.

All around them was orderly confusion, as counselors and kids unloaded horses, gathered up luggage, and said good-byes or hellos. As their station wagon came to the front of the line, Linda swept back her dark hair and put on her cowboy hat. Bob raked his fingers through his short blond hair.

Then a tall, lean man was standing beside their window. "I'm Tony Gordon," he said, "in charge of the intermediate riders. You're . . . ?"

"Bob and Linda Craig," Bob said.

"Okay, Bob and Linda." Tony opened their door. "Let's get your horses out."

They walked back to the trailer, opened the doors,

4

and set down the ramp. Tony said, "Bob, you take your horse first."

Bob backed Rocket out of the trailer, patting his neck to calm him down. Then Linda went in to get Amber. The golden horse snorted and tossed her spun-silk mane as if to say, "It's about time you got me out."

Linda stroked Amber's neck. "Getting bored back here?" she asked. "Well, you'll have lots of excitement in a second." She attached a lead rope to Amber's halter, unsnapped the crossties, and backed the horse out of the trailer.

Amber's hooves rang loudly against the ramp. She blinked for a second as she came into the sunlight. Then her ears went up and her eyes went wide as she took in this strange new place. The noise and movement unsettled her. She snorted and pranced around a little, her golden coat shining in the sun.

"That's a fine-looking animal," Tony Gordon said.

Linda thanked him, then patted Amber's neck. "Somebody's noticed you. Happy now?" She led Amber to stand beside Rocket.

Bronco and Doña had already unpacked the luggage. Now Bob's and Linda's bags stood with the other campers' gear, in neat rows guarded by a counselor.

"I suppose we'll have to move along," Doña said, coming over to the kids. She gently held her granddaughter by the shoulders and smiled. "Be—"

"I know, Doña," Linda said softly. "'Be good, be careful, and have fun.' I love you too," she added, returning her grandmother's grin.

Then Bronco grabbed Linda and gave her a bear hug. "You learn a lot here. And come back ready to teach me, okay?"

Linda nodded, blinking back the tears that had gathered in her eyes. "I'll miss you, Bronco."

Just then a sharp nudge from Amber made Linda stumble into her grandfather. They both laughed.

"All right. I get the message. I know you'll be here to keep me company, Amber," Linda said. She kissed the velvety soft muzzle that Amber had shoved under her arm.

Bob and Linda waved good-bye as Bronco and Doña got back in the station wagon and drove off. Then Tony Gordon came over and handed them each a slip of paper. "These are your assignments. Bob, Pete Dorfman will lead you to your stable, Stallion City." He pointed to a young counselor standing with two other boys with horses. "Linda, go with Ronnie Ryberg to Filly Alley."

Linda turned to see a short girl, about sixteen years

old with curly, dark hair, starting to lead three other girls and horses down a wide pathway. She quickly caught up as they reached four barns laid out in a square with a sandy open area in the middle. Ronnie led them to a barn with a large sign that read "Filly Alley."

"Nice," Linda said, pausing just inside the door. It was a beautiful stable, with eight good-size box stalls on each side of the center aisle.

There was an even better surprise when she led Amber into her stall. "Hey, there's a door on the other side!"

Linda opened the top half of the door and saw a grassy paddock outside. Amber nudged in beside her, eager to see. Linda laughed. "I'll leave the top open so you can enjoy the view." She checked that the bottom of the outside door was bolted, then went through the inside door and bolted that.

Ronnie had assembled the other girls. "I'd better explain about the rules," she said. "Mr. Harrington's very fussy. If you break the rules, you'll get demerits. If you get fifty demerits, you can be disqualified from the competitions."

Linda nodded. She knew from her camp brochure that there were three major competitions—a gymkhana, or horse meet with racing, which would be held in a week; an endurance ride on the next-to-last day of camp; and finally, the horse show on the last day.

"The important rules are to keep your horse's bedding clean, keep the stall door closed and bolted, and keep your halter hanging on the hook."

Ronnie led the way to the tack room, where she assigned each girl a locker. "You'll keep brushes, currycombs, hoof picks, and any other equipment in here. Anything left lying around will go to the lost and found. If you want it back, you'll have to take demerits."

The campers glanced at each other. This place was serious. Back home, on the rare times Linda left anything out, she just got a scolding from Mac, Rancho del Sol's foreman.

"Okay, let's get your luggage and find your bunks," Ronnie said. "You may want to change into some old clothes." She grinned down at her own creased shirt, worn jeans, and scuffed boots. "We have work to do."

The girls had barely enough time to get their bags, find their bunkhouses, and change before Ronnie turned up again. She led everyone back toward Filly Alley.

Linda turned to a short girl with bright red hair. "What kind of work are we supposed to be doing?"

"The worst," the girl whispered back. "Loading hay. They make us do it every year on the first day." She winked. "You'd think they'd at least have the camp ready, with all our folks are paying. I'm Mary Ryan, by the way."

"I'm Linda Craig. Mary, do they expect us to move all the bales by ourselves?"

"There'll be counselors, and they'll bring in some boys, too. Don't worry, it'll be fun."

Getting bale after bale of hay into the hayloft was work, but Mary was right. It was fun, too. Linda got to meet all of the girls who'd be staying in her bunkhouse and a bunch of other campers as well.

Bob was there, laughing as he raked wisps of hay out of his hair with his fingers. A lot of hay and straw swirled in the air as the kids moved hay bales around.

"I don't want my horse breathing this stuff!" Linda heard a voice say. Turning, she saw a girl climbing down the hayloft ladder—a girl who seemed totally out of place among the ragtag workers. Although she was only a teenager, her mane of long auburn hair made her look like a fashion model. And her shiny black boots, perfectly fitted riding pants, and spotless shirt stood out against the rumpled jeans and T-shirts around her.

9

"I thought we were supposed to wear old clothes," Linda puffed as she pushed at a bale of hay.

Ronnie Ryberg overheard her. "For Laurie Cavendish, those probably *are* old clothes. Her family owns about half of downtown Denver."

"Does her horse have a problem with the hay?" Linda asked.

"Her horse is a fancy Thoroughbred," Ronnie said. "We don't want any common old *hay* falling on her."

Laurie returned, brushing hay off her shoulders. Ronnie and Linda both hid smiles. "Now Lady Jane is safe outside," Laurie said, coming over to help the girls move the hay across the floor.

Tony Gordon was supervising how the hay was stacked. "We need some help to get this bale standing up," he called.

His voice was drowned out by noise from outside—a neigh, then two horses wildly, angrily whinnying.

The bale dropped to the floor as Laurie turned around. "That's Lady Jane!"

Linda was already running for the ladder. "That's *my* horse—Amber!"

2 ♦♦♦♦

Linda went flying down the ladder, with Laurie right after her. What was wrong with Amber? Why was that other horse whinnying?

Linda ran to Amber's stall, opened the door, and stopped in her tracks, almost getting knocked over by Laurie. The other door, the one that led to the paddock, was wide open.

Together they rushed outside, and now it was Laurie's turn to gasp. Just as they passed the doorway, they saw Amber kick out her rear hooves at Lady Jane. The Thoroughbred leapt back, whinnying, her eyes flaring.

Linda expected Amber to whinny, too, to paw the ground or toss her head. But after Lady Jane jumped back, Amber stood very still, almost rigid. She kept her back to the Thoroughbred, her head down and her ears flat against her skull. Only an occasional shudder rippled along Amber's ribs. Linda drew a silent breath. If the other horse came close again . . .

As if on cue, Lady Jane headed for Amber, sticking her neck way out.

Sure enough, Amber kicked at her again.

"Has your horse gone out of its mind?" Laurie demanded.

"Stop shouting," Linda hissed at her. "You're only upsetting Amber."

Laurie stared at her. "Your horse is trying to kill mine!"

"Just keep an eye on *your* horse." Linda stepped out into the paddock. Very softly she said, "Hey, Amber, I'm here. It's okay now. Nobody's going to hurt you."

Clucking quietly, Linda stepped closer and closer to her horse.

"What got you all excited, huh, girl?"

Amber's head was still down, but she was looking at Linda. Coming closer, Linda was able to get hold of the mare's halter. She gently stroked Amber, running her hand down the horse's nose.

At last, Amber calmed down. Linda breathed a sigh of relief. "Maybe you should get your horse," she said to Laurie.

The other girl moved quickly toward Lady Jane.

Amber's head shot up, and her eyes rolled, following Laurie.

"Hey, hey," Linda said to her horse. "Calm down." Amber snorted and nudged Linda's shoulder. The mare's fear and anger were fading away. Very gently Linda reached up and scratched the horse's ears.

Now Laurie had her horse, too.

"That was a nice job of calming those horses down. What was going on in the first place?" a voice asked from behind them.

They turned to find Hank Harrington standing in the open stall door, with most of the other hay loaders right behind him.

"I left Lady Jane out here to keep her away from all that hay in the air," Laurie said. "The paddock was empty. Then this girl's horse got out of its stall and attacked Lady Jane."

Hank turned to Linda. His voice was stern. "You left the outside stall door open? We have a major rule here—"

"Both doors were bolted when I left," Linda said quickly. "Maybe Amber was able to open it with her lips. She does that sometimes."

"I bet she does," Laurie scoffed.

"My sister's telling the truth," Bob said. "I've seen Amber do it."

"I still don't understand what set Amber off like that," Linda said, patting her horse. "She never—" As her hand rested on the mare's shoulder, Amber suddenly flinched. "Wait a second—look at this swelling!"

She brought Amber over to Hank Harrington and pointed. "That's a bite mark—there on the shoulder."

Laurie licked her lips. "Lady Jane must have been defending herself," she said.

"That's a weird way to defend herself from a kicking horse," Linda said angrily. "Amber had her back to Lady Jane when she was kicking—but this bite is in *front,* on her shoulder. I think Amber came over to Lady Jane, and your horse bit her. That's what started the trouble."

Hank looked from Laurie to Bob to Linda. "We'll have to wire that door shut," he finally said. "I don't want this happening again. Linda, I'll have someone take a look at your horse." Then he turned to the others. "Now let's get back to work and forget about the whole thing."

As Linda spent the rest of the afternoon shoving

bales of hay around, she couldn't help noticing Laurie Cavendish glaring at her. It looked as if one person wasn't about to forget what had happened.

When they finished storing the hay, all Linda wanted was a hot shower. There was still the bunkhouse to set up, though.

It was a simple place but very clean and cool. There were two rows of three metal bunks each. Next to each bunk was a wooden cubby. In between the bunks were small windows with red-and-white-checked curtains. At the far end of the cabin were a shower room and a lavatory.

The girls had already chosen their bunks, but there was still the job of making them up and unpacking, supervised by a counselor named Vivian Scott, whose bed was in an alcove near the door.

Linda had a middle bunk. Her right-hand neighbor was red-haired Mary Ryan. On the left was a girl with a blond ponytail named Fran Williams. The bunk across from Linda had been chosen by Janey Paulsen, a girl with light brown hair cut in bangs. Tall, thin Pamela Addabo had the bunk opposite Mary, and a slightly chubby girl named Kate Fraser was opposite Fran.

As they put their stuff away, Linda wondered how

Pamela would ever fit all the things from her luggage into one cubby. Her shirts alone would fill it. Her mane of dark curls bobbing as she laughed, Pam solved the problem by hiding a bag full of jeans and several pairs of boots under her bunk. Mary kept everyone laughing with stories of the last season at the camp. She considered herself an "old hand," since she'd been there for two years.

Just as they finished, the dinner bell rang.

Linda and her bunkmates had no problem finding the dining hall—they just followed the stream of hungry kids. After some of the outrageous horror stories Mary had told about camp food, Linda was wondering what to expect. She knew each bunkhouse had its own table. Where would Bob be sitting?

As she headed for the door, Linda nearly bumped into Laurie Cavendish. She looked at the beautiful girl for a moment, wondering what to say. Laurie just moved straight ahead, staring right through Linda as if she were invisible.

Well, Linda thought, looking after her, the brochure said the next two weeks would be challenging.

Ronnie Ryberg came up and steered Linda toward her bunk's table. "You got the big hello from Laurie, I see. Don't judge all the C.I.T.s by her."

"All the whats?" Linda asked.

"C.I.T.s—counselors in training. We work here, Laurie and I." Ronnie shrugged. "Even though I don't know why she bothers. Her folks could buy the camp for her, so she gets the best that money can buy—horses, tack, instructors. Part of her family tradition, I guess. Her mother was a champion rider when she was younger."

Linda glanced over toward Laurie. "I guess she must be a great rider."

"Here's our table," Ronnie said abruptly, closing the subject of Laurie Cavendish.

Ronnie sat at the table, talking to the other kids and drawing all of them into the conversation. One thing they all had in common was a love of horses. Only Mary had been to Crystal Valley before, the others hadn't. Janey started asking questions about the camp. She seemed to be taking some of Mary Ryan's tall tales a little too seriously.

"You'll get the whole lowdown on the camp in a second." Ronnie nodded toward the center of the room, where Hank Harrington stood. He clapped his hands loudly three times, calling for silence. When the dining hall was quiet, he picked up his clipboard.

"Well, you've met me as the camp director," he

said, "but I wear another hat. I'm also the advanced riding instructor. Half of the team, actually. Nancy Bauer is the nice person." Nancy, a trim young woman with light brown hair, got up and waved.

"Then there's Tony Gordon, who teaches the intermediates. He moves people up so fast, we need two people to take care of his graduates." Linda recognized the tall, lean counselor who had supervised the unloading of her horse.

"Stan O'Neill instructs the beginners—we saved the oldest and wisest for the younger kids." Stan had a round face, a bald head with a fringe of gray curls, and a gray beard.

"Our crafts and entertainment director is Vivian Scott. She runs the sing-alongs and skits and is always happy to discover a new star." Linda's blond bunk counselor got up to wave to the other campers.

"George Davis is our W.S.I.—our water safety instructor. After a hard day in the saddle, you'll be pretty happy to hit the pool." George was a young, sandy-haired guy who popped up quickly to wave to everyone.

"I almost forgot we won't be riding every minute of every day," Linda whispered to Ronnie.

"You'll be riding plenty," Ronnie whispered back.

"And then there are our counselors in training.

Watch out for the C.I.T.s—they're tougher than the regular counselors."

"Don't believe it," Ronnie said, laughing, as she and a dozen other kids stood up. Linda noticed that Laurie Cavendish didn't wave to the crowd.

"I saved the most important people for last," Hank went on. "Mrs. Thompson, our cook, and her kitchen staff. Better start clapping now, or we'll never get supper."

The crowd laughed and applauded. As the noise died down, Hank started talking again. "When you applied for camp, you told us what riding level *you thought* you were at. Tomorrow you'll ride, and we'll tell you what level *we know* you're at."

He smiled as everyone laughed again, but his face was very serious as he continued. "We raise the flag every morning at eight o'clock. No one is to be late—not even one minute. Then we'll head over to the indoor arena and you can show us your riding.

"We expect everyone to be properly attired. If you ride Western, that means cowboy boots, jeans, chaps, shirt, gloves, and hat. If you ride English, it means boots, britches, shirt, tie, jacket, gloves, and hunt cap. Anyone not properly attired doesn't ride."

He paused for a moment to let that sink in. "By now, each of you has been shown where to keep your tack and equipment. You should also know that you're responsible for keeping your horses perfectly groomed.

"Now you know the rules. And you should know that if you break these rules, you'll earn demerits. Get fifty demerits, and you're out of the competitions."

He paused again, and when he continued, his voice was softer. "I don't enjoy giving demerits. But I hate it a lot more when horses or riders get hurt because of sloppiness. So remember the rules, and we can all have a great time in the next two weeks. Now, dig in!"

Supper looked delicious, and everyone had worked up an appetite. For a while, the table was quiet. After the apple pie dessert, Vivian Scott stood up. "At seven-thirty tonight, we'll be lighting the campfire, and then there'll be a sing-along. Remember to bring your voices."

"And a warm sweatshirt," Ronnie told the girls. "It gets chilly after dark."

After Nancy Bauer took them on a tour of the camp and they spent a little time with their horses, they all headed back to the bunkhouse. Long shadows were coming from the mountains by the time Linda got back to the mess hall.

The campfire was hard to miss. Orange sparks flew high into the darkening sky from the sandy clearing in the center of the camp. Linda took a deep breath. Even at this distance, she could taste the sharp, smoky smell of burning pine. The flickering light showed the circle of kids and counselors gathered round the campfire.

Vivian Scott sat tuning a guitar. Stan O'Neill and Ronnie Ryberg had guitars, too. They joined in strumming as Vivian began singing "Red River Valley." Voices began to sing as well, then Linda heard a harmonica. She looked across the fire to see Bob playing. He winked at her.

The rest of the evening was spent singing old cowboy songs, until the campfire was a pile of embers and Linda was doing more yawning than singing.

"I think we should call it a night," Vivian finally said. "Bob, do you think you could handle 'Taps' on that harmonica?"

Bob stood up and started playing the haunting melody. Somehow, it sounded even sadder when a coyote up on the mountain joined in with a howl.

Then the crowd broke up and headed for the different bunkhouses. Linda joined Mary and Kate as they walked through the doorway. "That was great!" Mary said. "I could have stayed at the fire all night."

"Only one thing could be better," Kate said, plumping down on her bunk. "A pillow fight!" Even as she said those words, she had her pillow flying at Mary.

Mary ducked, and the pillow hit Linda. She tossed it at Kate, who promptly flung it back. Soon the air was filled with giggles and flying pillows as the rest of the girls entered and joined in.

Ronnie Ryberg stepped into the bunkhouse, grabbing a pillow in midair. "Just what we need," she said. "A bunk full of behavior problems." Then she laughed and threw the pillow at Linda. A moment later, the fight was back in full swing.

Then Laurie Cavendish appeared in the doorway. "Stop this!" she yelled. Her eyes fell on Linda, who was holding the pillow Ronnie had thrown.

"You'd be better off saving your energy," Laurie said. "You'll be riding hard tomorrow."

Linda dropped the pillow. It looked like the next two weeks would be more of a challenge than she'd thought.

3 ◆◆◆◆

The next morning at the flag raising, Linda glanced around curiously at the other campers. Some looked a little tired—either they weren't used to getting up early, or they hadn't slept well. After Laurie's comment the night before, Linda had surprised herself by drifting right off to sleep. Maybe moving all those bales of hay had something to do with it.

After breakfast, as the time for the riding demonstrations came closer, she found herself almost impatient—eager to get started.

Soon enough, she had her chance. Linda was among the first riders called at the arena.

"Let's show them what we can do, Amber!" She swung up into the saddle, clicked her tongue, and squeezed Amber's sides with her legs to signal her to move forward.

Linda had only gone three yards when she heard Hank Harrington shout, "Linda Craig—get down off that horse!"

Reining Amber to a halt, Linda dismounted and turned to face Hank. Her heart was thudding. Hank had made lots of suggestions to the other riders before Linda, but he hadn't told anyone to get off a horse!

"Linda," Hank said, "what's the proper riding attire for Western class?"

"Boots, jeans, chaps, shirt, and hat," Linda replied.

"And?" Hank demanded.

Linda was suddenly aware of her bare hands. "And gloves," she said.

"Where are yours?" Hank asked.

Linda pulled the gloves out of her back pocket. "I—I'm not used to wearing them," she said.

"I suppose you're used to calluses when your horse decides to take the reins?" Hank wasn't really asking for an answer, and Linda didn't give one. "Or maybe you think that can't happen to you," he continued. "Well, it can. And I won't have it happen to any of my campers. Understand?"

Linda's brown eyes grew large. She cleared her throat and said, "Yes."

"All right," Hank said, his tone still harsh. "Go to the end of the line. Ronnie, five demerits for Linda Craig."

As Linda led Amber from the arena, she felt her cheeks burn with embarrassment. She knew that everyone in the stands was staring at her, and she kept her eyes on the ground.

Ronnie walked outside with her. "Don't worry too much about it, okay?" she said. "Nobody gets through two weeks without any demerits. You just got yours out of the way early." As she headed back to the arena, Mary Ryan came hurrying up.

"You just saved my life, you know," she said.

"I did?" Linda asked, bewildered.

Mary nodded. "You were ahead of me in line. That gave me just enough time to run back to the cabin and get my gloves."

In spite of herself, Linda had to smile. "Well, I'm glad I was able to help," she said. "But the next time, it's your turn."

Mary laughed and ran back into the arena. Linda stayed where she was, still feeling humiliated. Amber came up and nudged her shoulder. She wanted to be scratched. "Not now, Amber." Linda sighed. "I don't feel like it. I just feel like going home."

Amber stepped back, raised her head, and tossed

her cream-colored mane. Then she let out a long, high whinny.

Linda shook her head as she looked at Amber's bright, shining eyes. With a horse like this, how could she give up? "You're right," she said. "I'm acting like a baby, not a rider. I've just got a lot to learn."

The least Linda could do was take the time to scratch the horse behind her ears.

Once again, she heard her name called from inside the arena. Hoping she looked more confident than she felt, Linda led Amber back into the building, pulled on her gloves, mounted, and rode into the show ring.

She followed Hank's barked instructions: "Walk your horse. Half-turn. Now a figure eight."

Linda felt tense as she started following Hank's orders. But as Amber went smoothly through every movement, Linda's confidence began to grow.

"Keep your heels down," Hank's voice rang out. "Now trot through the figure eight. Then return to the rail."

Amber responded to Linda's signals flawlessly. As they made the final circle of the ring, Linda couldn't hold back a smile of pride. Amber moved like a dream.

"All right, Linda," Hank said. He checked his

watch. "Campers, walk your horses to cool them off. Untack, and take care of the grooming. After lunch, assignments will be posted on the bulletin board outside the dining hall."

Linda had never seen so many people eat lunch so quickly. When she finished, she found a mob clustered around the bulletin board. Linda finally reached the board, to find her name on the list for the Desperados—the intermediate riders. At least her mistake hadn't gotten her demoted to the Colts, or beginners.

Intermediate was the highest she could reach at her age. Campers had to be fourteen even to be considered for the advanced class, the High Riders.

Linda looked for her brother's name and found it on the advanced list—right under Laurie Cavendish.

Before she headed back to the bunkhouse, Linda picked up the schedule for the Desperados. They would meet in the indoor arena to practice riding technique every morning from ten to noon. Every afternoon from one to three there would be games practice in the outdoor arena. And from four to five, they'd have horsemanship and care and grooming lessons.

During their spare time, campers had a choice of crafts, swimming, or recreational activities.

27

"I'm tired just reading this schedule," Mary said.

"There won't be much time to get bored," Linda said.

"Or homesick," Mary added, with a look at Linda. "Why don't I show you the swimming hole? I have to decide between swimming and crafts for afternoon 'individual choice time.' And I wonder what the 'special late-afternoon event' will turn out to be."

They found out at four o'clock, when the counselors gathered the campers together and told them to saddle up. "We're hitting the trail!" Hank Harrington said.

A trail ride! Linda hurried over to Filly Alley to get Amber all tacked out. She'd been hoping for a chance to explore some of the mountain trails, and now she'd get it.

Amber quickly caught the excitement from the hubbub of the campers. She thrust her head over the stall door, wanting to know what was going on, and took little prancing steps as Linda saddled her up.

"Take it easy," Linda told her horse. "Nobody's leaving without us." She led Amber out of the stable.

A couple of moments later, Mary came out with her horse, Red. "This is going to be great," she said.

"It's kind of late in the day," Linda said as they

mounted. "What are we supposed to do about supper?"

Mary just smiled mysteriously. "You'll see."

By now, just about everyone was ready. Hank Harrington rode among them on a big gray, inspecting people.

"Got your gloves?" Mary asked.

"I think from now on, I'll just wear them all the time," Linda answered.

The head counselor came by and gave a small, approving nod. "You'll be riding with Ronnie," he said. "She's helping Tony with the Desperados."

Linda felt a little jolt of surprise. She'd just figured that she could ride with Bob and maybe a few new friends. Instead, she'd have a counselor riding herd over her. Camp had a lot more rules than she'd expected.

As they set off, she saw Bob in the distance, riding with Laurie Cavendish, of all people. Still, Laurie seemed to be smiling as Bob had to rein in Rocket's enthusiastic rush to begin. Linda was riding with Mary, Ronnie, and a couple of girls from her bunkhouse, Pam and Janey. There was also a younger girl named Ellen Lake who had made it into the Desperados. She had about a million freckles, and was very excited to be riding with the "big kids."

The trail took a lot of twists and turns as it worked its way into the foothills. Then came a straight, steep section that took them to the top of a hill, high above the valley.

"This part is really a beginner's trail," Ronnie told them. "But it gives you a great view of the whole ranch."

As they reached the top of the hill, Linda saw what Ronnie meant. They could see the whole valley spread out below them. The ranch buildings looked like brightly painted toys. Linda turned to look back down the trail, where Nancy Bauer, Stan O'Neill, and a bunch of C.I.T.s were carefully shepherding the Colts along.

The trail ride went along at a leisurely pace—as Hank Harrington said, they were riding, not racing. This was a different kind of trail from the ones Linda knew on Rancho del Sol. She was used to desert riding. Even when they went up into the California mountains, it was dry country. Here she saw grass, gorges cut by mountain springs, and everywhere the grayish green of sagebrush. The sweet smell of the sage came to them with every breath.

The trail led them to a small stream. As they splashed through, some of the horses shied. Then they set off to top another rise, where they found—of all things—an old-fashioned mailbox on a post.

"Okay, guys," Ronnie said. "Each of you will open the box—while still on your horse."

"What's this for?" Linda wanted to know.

"You didn't think we were just going out for fun, did you?" the C.I.T. asked with a grin. "This is part of the practice for the trail-ride competition. You'll find all sorts of things to test your horsemanship along the way—streams to ford, gates to go through, fences to jump, and sometimes a mailbox. Who'll try first?"

Ellen brought her horse, Wonder, forward. She leaned over to flip the mailbox door open. It fell down with a loud squeak.

Wonder snorted and shied away, nearly sending Ellen out of her saddle.

"Now close it."

Clinging tightly with her knees, Ellen tried to bring her horse back to the box. But the noise had spooked Wonder—she wouldn't go near the mailbox.

"More of a test than it looks, isn't it?" Ronnie asked. "Don't worry about it—we'll be practicing."

None of the horses liked the mailbox, not even Amber. But at least she came back to let Linda close the door.

They set off again. Another half-hour's riding took them into a miniature canyon carved by a wider-than-usual spring. The lower end even had a small lake, where a rockslide had dammed up the water flow.

"It's beautiful!" said Linda.

"Even better than that." Mary kicked her heels into Red's sides to get a little more speed. "It's super!"

Ahead of them, between the trees, they could see dancing flames—campfires. As they came closer, they found the fires blazing away in carefully constructed pits lined with stones. Tony Gordon was directing traffic, sending the different groups to picket lines set up among the trees. Campers were also allowed to take their horses down to the stream for a drink of water.

Amber patiently waited her turn and thankfully drank some of the cool, clear mountain water. A couple of kids went a little farther upstream to taste the water themselves.

"It's *cold!*" Mary reported, shivering.

After they'd tied up the horses and made them comfortable, Linda, Mary, and Ellen headed for the campfires. Mrs. Thompson and some of her helpers were handing out hot dogs and long sticks.

"You'll cook for yourselves tonight, kids!" Mrs. Thompson said, grinning at them.

They had a good time, standing close enough to feel the heat of the crackling flames, roasting their own franks. Ellen managed to catch her stick on fire. It broke, dropping the hot dog in the middle of the fire.

For a second, the young girl looked ready to cry, but Mrs. Thompson had come prepared with extras. Ellen soon had a finished frank on her bun, with double mustard and relish.

The camp cooks hadn't been goofing off, either. Linda had noticed that one of the fire pits was just a pile of banked coals. Now some staff members dug carefully under the embers to reveal a layer of corn ears, roasting Indian-fashion in their own husks.

With butter, salt, and pepper, they made a delicious feast. Then Vivian Scott brought out her guitar, and there were a few songs as the kids toasted marshmallows.

The sun was just beginning to set as Hank Harrington called the campers together. "We'll be heading back to the ranch now—no sense riding in the dark. High Riders, get your horses first."

A few moments later, it was the Desperados' turn to get their horses. Linda was already close to the picket line where Amber was tied. She quickly headed for her horse.

As she approached, she heard a horse give an angry snort, then a voice yelling, "Keep that stupid horse away. She tried to snap at me!"

Linda recognized the voice—it was Ronnie Ryberg's.

"Lady Jane wouldn't do that." Linda recognized this voice, too—it belonged to Laurie Cavendish.

"Oh, no, any horse that belongs to you would be too perfect," Ronnie said sarcastically. "I've got news for you—that nag doesn't know the rules."

"Then you two should get on beautifully," Laurie said. "You ignore the rules around here all the time."

Right then, Amber heard Linda coming and whinnied a greeting.

"Someone's there," Ronnie whispered. "Quiet down."

"Sure," Laurie whispered back. "But this isn't over."

4 ◆◆◆◆

Linda noticed that Ronnie was quiet for the whole ride back to camp. If she wasn't giving some sort of instruction to her campers, she didn't say a word.

Ahead of them in the gathering dusk, Linda could see Laurie Cavendish's stiff, angry back. The other campers didn't seem to notice. But the horses were more aware of the strained atmosphere. Amber fidgeted all the way home, turning back to look at Linda as if to ask, "What's wrong?"

"C'mon, Amber. Knock it off." Linda pulled back on the reins.

"If you can't handle your horse in the dark, I'll lead her back," Ronnie growled.

Linda glared at Ronnie's back. Whether the counselor realized it or not, *she* was the reason Amber was acting skittish.

While they stabled the horses, the silence between Ronnie and Laurie could have been cut with a knife. Ronnie snapped at Pam, and Laurie gave Kate a long look, just daring her to try starting a pillow fight that night.

Everyone went to bed feeling subdued. Linda had a hard time getting to sleep.

The next morning Linda got to meet her instructor. She'd actually met Tony Gordon when she'd arrived —he'd been the tall, lean counselor who had supervised the unloading of the horses. This morning, though, she *really* got to know him. He was in his early twenties and an excellent instructor—a lot of fun, but his standards were high.

"We'll start today's lesson moving at a walk," he told the intermediate riders. "Just start circling the ring."

The kids started around the edge of the ring in a slow procession.

"Feels like a slow-motion film, doesn't it?" Tony smiled at the campers as they slowly moved past him. "But I'll tell you something. My eagle eyes have found lots of riding problems at this pace—you don't have to be going faster. It saves a lot of wear and tear on the instructor, too—I don't have to chase you as hard."

That got a laugh from the kids.

"So," Tony said, "let's begin. You guys think you know all about walking? I want to see you spiral in at the walk."

The campers left the rail and started circling in raggedly.

"Miss Lake," Tony called out to young Ellen. "Guide with the legs, not the hands. Stop hauling on those reins."

Ellen Lake stiffened in her saddle. But she did guide her horse through the next turn by the pressure of her heel on the horse's side.

As the parade continued, the spiral became more and more ragged. Some riders were moving too slowly, others too fast. Finally, one horse crowded the one in front of him. The crowded horse, a good-size bay, snorted and kicked at the horse behind it.

"Hold it!" Tony's voice cut across the hubbub. "Mr. Vine, I notice your horse likes to kick. But I don't see a red ribbon on his tail to warn other riders."

"He—he doesn't kick, usually," Charlie Vine admitted as the riders headed back to the rail. "Not unless people come too close. I didn't—"

"That's a five-demerit 'I didn't.'" Tony looked his campers up and down. "So, this is the group that knows all about riding at the walk. I'd hate to see how you'd have done at a trot—or faster."

He clapped his hands sharply. "Okay, people. Now, one at a time, I'd like to see you try some half-turns—this time at the walk."

The practice became more interesting. Tony found more to say about each rider's performance—every rider except Linda and Amber. They performed perfectly.

"Not bad," he said. "Miss Craig, let's see you try a figure eight. At a canter."

Some of the kids looked at one another a little nervously.

Linda rode to the center of the corral, trying to hide a smile. This was something she and Amber had practiced to perfection.

They set off through the first loop of the figure. Then came the tricky part. Halfway through, Amber had to do a flying change—change the leg she led off on—and do it in midair. Miss the timing, and Amber would break step.

The moment came. Linda shifted her weight—and Amber performed with the grace of a champion.

"Very nice, Miss Craig," Tony said. "Could you take it up a notch?"

Linda glanced over at Tony, who only smiled at her.

"Knock yourself out," he said.

"Okay, Amber, let's show him." Amber speeded up. They headed for the center again—and again, Amber came through with flying colors.

"Thank you, Miss Craig. You've shown everybody else what to do. Maybe the rest can go back to circles."

The classes weren't easy. Tony found a way to challenge each of his students. But Linda threw herself into the classes with enthusiasm. She tried to follow all of Tony's advice. Even a couple of days showed her what a difference it made in her riding.

On one of her "free choice" hours, Linda decided not to swim. She went over to the indoor arena to watch her brother's lesson.

Hank Harrington stood in the center of the ring, barking instructions as his students rode by. Although Bob looked grim, he followed the instructions to the letter.

The next couple of riders didn't do so well. They seemed to be so rattled by Hank's commands that they rode like beginners.

After them came Laurie Cavendish. She and Lady

Jane gracefully threaded their way through the routine. They also worked in total silence—Hank didn't say a word.

Linda sat back, amazed. It was as if Hank Harrington had left the arena and a silent look-alike had taken his place.

Next, Ronnie Ryberg entered the show ring, and Hank shouted instructions at her nearly nonstop.

But, Linda thought, he was correcting only minor points in an almost perfect performance. Linda had never seen anyone ride as well as Ronnie. The tiny girl was not as smooth as Laurie. She was tighter, moving more abruptly, but she was on the mark for every move.

Across the ring, Linda saw Laurie and Bob sitting on their horses, watching Ronnie intently. Linda figured she understood Laurie's eagle eye. She was looking for something to criticize. Linda couldn't understand why Bob was watching so closely, though.

Hank called out the name of the next rider and put him through his paces. Linda again noticed Laurie watching. The beautiful auburn-haired girl leaned over and touched Bob on the elbow, saying something as the rider faltered.

Linda also noticed Ronnie off to one side, walking her horse and giving Laurie a dirty look. Bob just grinned and nodded.

Linda couldn't believe it. Could Laurie really be making fun of the other riders? With Bob just listening?

She couldn't hang around to find out. As Hank Harrington summoned his next victim, Linda looked at her watch. It was time for Horsemanship.

Tony Gordon held his class in a paddock outside one of the stables. Today he was lecturing on how important grooming was for young horses. "It's not just good for their looks, it relaxes the horses and helps them grow into control of their bodies."

He demonstrated on his horse, and then had all the Desperados work on their own.

Amber loved the attention. She rolled her head from side to side for Linda to scratch behind her ears.

Linda's interest in the class was halfhearted. She couldn't get the picture of the High Riders' class out of her mind—Ronnie glaring, Laurie whispering in Bob's ear.

After classes ended that evening, Linda caught up with Bob outside the dining hall. "I have to talk to you," she said to him. "Have you noticed anything strange going on?"

"Like what?" Bob asked, surprised.

"Wel-l-l, I'm not exactly sure," Linda admitted. "But I think something funny is going on between Ronnie Ryberg and Laurie Cavendish."

Briefly, she outlined the incident of the pillow fight and the confrontation on the evening of the trail ride. "They're students with you, as well as counselors," she said. "I just wondered what you thought of them."

Bob just shrugged. "They're both great riders— better than I am, right now. Ronnie loves to compete. And Laurie just *rides* so perfectly. At least they don't have Hank breathing down their necks."

"How do they get along in class?" Linda asked.

Again, Bob shrugged. "So, Laurie and Ronnie don't get along. Nobody gets along with everybody. You'll only be here with them for two weeks—don't worry about it."

"They seem to take it a lot more seriously than most people," Linda said. "I just wondered if something had happened last summer that they were still mad about."

"I don't know. But I do know this." Bob leaned forward. "Try not to get caught between them. You don't have time to waste on that stuff. The gymkhana is only two days away."

Slowly Linda nodded. It was good advice, she knew. But she wasn't sure she could follow it.

5 ◆◆◆◆

On gymkhana day, Linda woke up with a bad case of butterflies. She always felt nervous before a competition. But today she felt extra jittery, as if something might go really wrong. She didn't know what. After all, this was just going to be a day of horse games. The campers would get to show off what they'd learned in the last week.

Still, there would be winners and losers, and that always put Linda a little on edge.

Linda had gotten up half an hour early to spend some extra time with Amber. She wanted her horse to look perfect for the day's activities. She knew Amber would enjoy a special session with the brush—not to mention another chance to have her ears scratched.

In spite of the early hour, there was someone already at work in Filly Alley—Laurie Cavendish.

Lady Jane was already cross-tied at the far end of the stable when Linda arrived.

Laurie was working with the body brush on her beautiful Thoroughbred. As Linda passed by on her way from the entrance to the tack room, Laurie didn't even seem to notice she was present. Laurie actually looked away when Linda was near.

Amber was peering over the door of her stall at the unexpected activity. But Lady Jane wasn't her favorite horse friend—Amber still remembered the nippy welcome the Thoroughbred had given her. Like horse, like rider? Linda wondered.

Linda went to her cubby in the tack room and got out her grooming gear. Then she headed back to Amber's stall.

Just then, Ronnie Ryberg came into the stable. "Hey, Laurie. Hi, Linda," the counselor said, leaning against the door to one of the stalls, and looked over at Laurie. "Getting your horse ready for the big day?"

Laurie didn't reply. She bent over her horse, still working.

Ronnie went on talking. "Everybody's been talking about how well you've done in class, Linda. They're saying you could wind up the star of the gymkhana. Wouldn't that be something? A real upset for some people who don't expect competition."

Ronnie gave a sidewise glance at Laurie. She might be talking to Linda, but that wasn't the only audience she was addressing.

Laurie looked startled at what Ronnie was saying, but only for a moment. She still didn't utter a word. She just worked over her horse.

"Well, I'm sure you'll do great," Ronnie said, waving good-bye. "Good luck, Linda."

"Um, thanks." Linda started walking toward Amber's stall. She realized that in spite of her brother's good advice, she'd wound up right between the two C.I.T.s. Ronnie had put her there.

Alone in the stable with the beautiful auburn-haired girl, Linda expected Laurie to do something to get even. But as usual, Laurie just ignored her. She continued to work on Lady Jane with her body brush.

Amber whinnied as Linda came into her stall. "Hope you're not having a bad day, too," Linda said to her horse.

Amber bent her head and extended her right hoof. She drew it back two times, counting for Linda.

Linda smiled at her. "Very good, but I didn't mean *two*. I meant *too*."

Amber pawed the ground four more times.

Linda laughed, which made her feel better. Still,

she couldn't get the recent scene out of her mind. Did people really think she had a chance to shine at the gymkhana? That was good news and bad. It made her feel proud, but it also added a couple of herds of butterflies to the thousand already fluttering inside her stomach.

Linda hardly ate anything at breakfast. The usual easygoing atmosphere at her table had vanished. Even Pam and Kate weren't fooling around as usual. It looked as though everyone from her bunkhouse was nervous—but all the girls loudly wished her good luck.

A lot of the Desperados stopped by to do the same thing. It seemed as though everyone in camp was expecting great things from her today. Charlie Vine came right out and said it. "Look, Linda, we'll all be riding, but you're the best in our group," he told her. "I know you'll show those High Riders that Desperados can ride."

On the way out of the dining hall, she saw Bob come out with Laurie Cavendish. "Hey, Linda," her brother called. "You know what the actors say— 'Break a leg.' "

"Thanks a lot." Linda laughed. "And good luck to you, too." Bob's good-natured teasing somehow brought everything back to normal. But Linda couldn't help noticing that Laurie didn't have a word to say.

Lost in her own thoughts, Linda went back to Filly Alley to spend the rest of the time before the competition getting Amber ready.

"I don't know why I'm worrying," Linda whispered to Amber when the time came to lead her to the arena. "I've got the best horse in camp, haven't I?"

Amber trotted up closer to Linda and nudged her hat so that it tipped forward over her eyes. Amber always seemed to know just when to make Linda laugh.

They walked up to the open end of the arena to watch the first event. The Colts were starting the gymkhana off with a bang, competing in an egg race. She decided to hitch Amber and sit in the bleachers to see how well the beginning riders did.

Stan O'Neill, the riding instructor for the Colts, explained the rules of the egg race. "There are four teams of five riders each. Each rider will be given a tablespoon with a hard-boiled egg on it. Each rider will have to walk his or her horse across the entire show ring without dropping the egg. Every unbroken egg will earn one point for that team."

It sounds easy, Linda thought. But she knew from

hard experience that it wasn't. You had to keep one eye on the far end of the arena and the other on the egg. If you looked only at the egg, you couldn't direct your horse. If you looked straight ahead, your hand would wobble and you'd lose the egg.

Hardest of all, you had to keep your legs and feet relaxed. If you tensed up, you could accidentally signal your horse into a trot—and the egg would fly off the spoon.

Stan hollered, "Go!" and the first five riders took off.

"Like a herd of turtles," muttered Mary Ryan, as she sat down next to Linda.

Just then the horse farthest from the stands suddenly broke into a trot. *Crunch!* went the egg. "O-h-h-h!" groaned the crowd.

The young rider trotted to the end of the ring so that the next rider on his team could begin.

Halfway to the goal, the rider nearest to the bleachers began to stare at his egg, forgetting to guide his horse. They crashed into the horse on their left. *Crunch!* went two more eggs.

In the end, twenty riders had carried seven unbroken eggs across the goal.

Tony Gordon strode out into the show ring. "Next event—after we get the scrambled eggs off the field—is the intermediate riders' barrel race," he said. "Come on, Desperados. Mount up!"

"That's us!" Mary Ryan shouted, jumping to her feet.

Linda had forgotten about her butterflies, but now they returned. She forced herself to walk out slowly to rejoin Amber.

"Here we go, girl," she whispered. Linda tested the girth and bridle, then reached for the gloves in her back pocket.

Not there! Frantic, she thought about where she could have left them. They must be in Amber's stall.

Linda retied Amber to a rail and raced back to the stable. There they were, on the floor of the stable. She picked them up and ran all the way back to the arena.

By the time she got back, the rest of the intermediate riders had led their mounts inside.

The only rider around was Laurie Cavendish in her beautiful caramel-colored jacket. Mary had told Linda that the High Riders usually showed up just before they had to ride. But of course Laurie would start getting ready way before the final event. That was one of the ways she managed to look so perfect. As usual, Laurie didn't look up at Linda. She was busy braiding Lady Jane's mane.

As Linda entered the arena, she heard someone

call, "Good luck!" She turned and saw Ronnie Ryberg leaning against the door frame.

"Thanks!" Linda said. "I'll need all the luck I can get."

Once inside, she watched the rider ahead of her as he skidded around the first barrel and rode toward the next one. She concentrated on spotting and mentally correcting his mistakes—not easy with the other campers yelling and clapping.

In the barrel race, the horse had to make very sharp turns, and the rider had to maintain just the right balance.

Poor Charlie Vine didn't get it right. His horse staggered and brushed against one of the barrels. Charlie hung his head as he finished.

Hank looked at his clipboard. "Linda Craig!" he called.

For just a second, Linda felt a flash of terror. Then she became perfectly calm.

It was time to ride!

Linda swung up into the saddle and eased Amber forward. She paused for a moment and ran through the entire race in her mind.

Then she took a deep breath and rolled her shoulders to relax them. She whispered excitedly, "Let's go, girl." Amber stepped out.

She headed for the barrels at full speed. Linda reined her into the first turn, shifted her weight forward, and leaned to the inside.

But something was wrong!

Linda couldn't right herself again. She was slipping, falling sideways. She desperately reached up to grab Amber's mane. But her fall was too fast now. Amber's neck was out of reach.

Linda kicked her feet free from the stirrups.

All she could do was hold her breath and wait for the sharp impact with the hard-packed dirt.

6 ◆◆◆◆

Whoosh! All the air was forced from Linda's lungs. She lay on her back with her eyes closed, watching dots of color change from red to yellow and then white.

When she opened her eyes, large colorful shapes floated behind the dots. Linda squinted, and slowly her vision cleared. She could now make out the large shapes as Tony Gordon, Ronnie, and her brother.

Then Hank Harrington pushed his way forward. "Are you okay?" he asked, gently checking Linda over for injuries.

Linda winced at a couple of bruises, but otherwise seemed fine. Gentle hands helped her up, and Bob put his arm around her, supporting her.

"Amber," Linda said. Amber had been standing anxiously to the side. Now she nosed close, checking to see that Linda was all right. But Linda was staring at her horse. Amber's saddle was hanging over her left side!

Hank Harrington's eyes followed Linda's. "Miss Craig!" he said suddenly, his voice very loud. "You have a real knack for ignoring the basics. I didn't think I'd have to remind you to check your girth before you ride."

Linda stared at him, then back at Amber. She remembered checking the strap under Amber's belly before coming into the arena. Maybe the girth broke, she thought. She reached under the stirrup to check. No, the straps were fine. The girth was definitely loose!

"Ten demerits, and you're out of today's competition," Hank Harrington said, and started to walk back to the judges' stand.

"Mr. Harrington, I—" Linda started to tell him that she *had* checked the strap, but broke off. He probably wouldn't believe her.

She ran to catch up with him. "I'd like another chance," she said. "I know it won't count, but I'd like to try, anyway."

Hank Harrington looked down at her steadily. He seemed to soften, just a little. Then he gave her a curt nod. "All right," he said.

Linda adjusted the saddle, refastened the cinch, and checked it. Then she swung into the saddle, rode back to the starting point, and urged Amber into a lope.

When Linda shifted her weight as Amber went into the turn at the first barrel, her bruised muscles complained. But Linda was angry now, determined to show what she and Amber could do. They came within a fraction of an inch of the barrel, but never touched it. They came out of the turn ready for the next barrel.

Linda shifted her weight the opposite way for the next turn. Straighten, turn, straighten, turn—all moving as fast as a straight-out gallop. The whole arena was quiet now. The slightest miscalculation would rack them up. But their rhythms matched perfectly.

After the last barrel, Linda let Amber gallop to the end of the arena. It was only then that the other campers burst out cheering.

"Maybe we're not winners, but we've shown them," Linda whispered to her horse.

Linda looked up into the stands with an embarrassed grin. A movement off to the right caught her eyes. Someone had been sitting way up in the back seats. Now the lone figure was descending the stairs.

Her head was bent, and a mane of auburn hair hid her face, but Linda recognized the caramel-colored riding jacket of Laurie Cavendish.

Linda's smile dissolved. She thought back to how she'd checked Amber's girth, then run back to the stable for her gloves. When she returned, there had been only one horse and rider standing close to Amber.

"Laurie Cavendish," whispered Linda. Could she have loosened the girth?

By the time Linda had walked Amber out of the arena, she knew she couldn't accuse Laurie without proof. "But if it wasn't Laurie, who was it?" she asked herself.

Amber couldn't give any answer except to poke a cold nose against Linda's cheek. Linda reached up and threw her arms around Amber's neck. "We'll figure it out, girl." Linda hugged her hard. "Right now, though, I have to get back to the arena to watch Bob. I'll see you soon."

Mary Ryan was standing in the arena entrance when Linda returned. "Are you feeling all right?" Mary asked anxiously. "After that fall, I figured you'd want to head back to the bunkhouse and lie down."

Linda shook her head. "I don't want to miss Bob's

turn," she said. Climbing the stairs made her stiff muscles protest. She was glad that Mary came along.

By the time Linda and Mary took their seats, the first of the High Riders had started dressage. Watching a horse and rider work through a careful and precise routine was inspiring, Linda thought.

Laurie Cavendish was the fourth of the advanced riders to perform. Linda thought her riding was flawless, and yet something was missing from the performance. Laurie was going through the motions, but her heart wasn't in it.

Mary and lots of other kids applauded enthusiastically at the end of Laurie's routine. I guess I'm the only one who thinks that something is wrong, thought Linda.

After three more riders, it was Bob's turn. Linda sat up excitedly, eager for him to do well.

His performance was a disappointment. A free-and-easy Western rider, Bob was uncomfortable performing the very controlled English dressage moves. Rocket's response to his rider's commands wasn't sharp, either. He'd been schooled in English riding, but was confused at Bob's sudden change in style. Their routine was rough, uneven—not winning quality.

Bob finished his ride to polite applause. Linda could see, even from the fifth row of the bleachers, that he was unhappy with his performance. A few minutes later, though, when he slid onto the bleacher next to her, he was looking more relaxed. He didn't say anything about his ride, and Linda didn't bring it up.

When the competition was over, the prizes were announced. Tony Gordon read off the third, second, and first fastest times in the barrel race. Mary Ryan had taken first. After the redheaded girl took her bow, Hank held up his hand for silence.

"I have one other time to announce. As you know, Linda Craig was disqualified from the competition. But I think it's worth mentioning that her time was just seven-tenths of a second faster than Mary's."

Linda gasped. She would have won! She felt Bob pat her back and heard him say, "Way to go. Next week you'll take a ribbon for sure."

Then the dressage results were announced. Laurie took first. Bob hadn't even placed. Linda glanced at Bob as Laurie, unsmiling, accepted her award. Bob was trying to look enthusiastic, but Linda could see he was just covering up his disappointment.

Impulsively, Linda said, "Tomorrow's Sunday, and we've got a free day. Let's go for a trail ride."

Bob looked down at her and smiled. He knew that she was just trying to cheer him up, but he was willing to let her try. "Okay," he said. "But we'll need a counselor along. I suppose I can ask Laurie—"

"Don't worry about it," Linda cut him off quickly. "I know Ronnie Ryberg will go with us."

The next day after lunch, Linda and Ronnie met Bob at the head of the trail they'd chosen. They sat on their horses, looking out across a large meadow of waist-high grass shimmering gold in the warm afternoon sun.

Bob pulled his hat down on his head so that it was settled better. He patted Rocket and pulled back on the reins to quiet the horse's prancing.

Then he looked over at the girls, and the corners of his mouth curved in a wicked grin. He winked once and shouted, "On your mark, get set—go!"

Linda had been ready for him. On "Go," she squeezed Amber's sides with her knees, leaned forward in the saddle with her heels down, and took off.

After a week of schooling, Amber needed to run. Linda let her have her head. In no time, Amber's mane was streaming back in the breeze.

Linda could barely see with the wind stinging her

eyes. But she could hear Rocket pounding along just behind her, and Ronnie on her horse, coming up fast.

She imagined Bob leaning far over Rocket's neck, urging him to catch up with Amber. But Amber loved to race more than anything and hated any horse near her.

She lengthened her pace until Linda knew what it must be like to fly. Nothing existed now except the pounding of Amber's hooves and the wonderful gallop of the horse beneath her.

Amber didn't tire. Her pace never slackened. Up ahead, Linda could see the stand of aspens where the race would end. She turned in her saddle for just a moment to check out her lead.

In that split second, Linda missed seeing the low fence that bounded the meadow. It was hidden by the tall grass, but Amber saw it and began her approach, ready to jump.

The only problem was that Linda wasn't prepared to jump. Amber's takeoff flung her back in the saddle. And when Amber landed, Linda flopped forward, losing a stirrup and falling on her horse's neck. Amber slowed then—and the race was lost.

Linda watched Bob sail over the fence, streaking by. Then Ronnie flew past her, crouched over her horse, close on Rocket's heels. By the time Linda got Amber started again, Bob had reached the aspens, declaring himself the winner with a loud whoop.

They all dismounted and walked their horses to cool them down. Bob turned to Ronnie. "Why didn't you warn us about that fence? Somebody could have gotten hurt!"

"I thought you knew about it," Ronnie said defensively. She hadn't been doing her job, Linda realized. She'd gotten so wound up in the race that she'd forgotten everything else.

Linda swung up on the fence, sitting back and looking at the mountain peaks above them. "You shouldn't have yelled so loud when you rode past the finish, Bob. I'm not sure it was a real win."

"You're right," Bob admitted. "I didn't actually win as much as you lost."

"Thanks a lot."

"I'll tell you something about racing," Ronnie said. "Never turn around to see where the other riders are. You'll lose every time."

"You sound like Hank Harrington," Linda grumped. "And what's worse, you're right."

Laughing, Ronnie moved off to get her horse. But Linda was very serious when she said to Bob, "You know, somebody loosened my girth yesterday at the arena."

He looked at her in surprise. "You mean someone wanted you to fall?"

"Maybe I looked like a sack of potatoes going over that fence, but I know enough to check the cinch strap." Linda frowned. "I think someone wanted me to lose."

"Look, it had to be some kind of accident," Bob said. "Why would someone do that on purpose?"

"Suppose someone didn't like me—and my horse?"

Bob's lips drew together in a thin line. "Like who?"

Linda continued to look up at the mountains. "How about Laurie Cavendish?" she said. "I had to leave Amber alone and get my gloves. Laurie was right nearby—close enough to loosen the girth."

Bob shook his head. "I think you're wrong. I ride with Laurie a lot. She's unhappy about something, but I don't think she'd do anything mean." He shrugged. "I suppose I should be jealous of her. She's perfect all the time and I—I'm riding like a loser."

"How come? What's the problem?" Linda asked softly.

"Back home when we go riding, it's fun. But here,

people are always breathing down my neck. They have more rules than I ever heard of in my life." He frowned. "It's cramping my style. And when it's not fun to get on Rocket . . ."

Bob shook his head. "I'll tell you something. The only person who's been helping me is Laurie Cavendish. She doesn't go around yelling like Hank—she talks quietly. And when the other riders make the same mistakes I do, she makes me see what's wrong."

Linda nodded. So that's what Laurie had been doing that day in Bob's class.

"I know I won't do well in the big show next week," Bob went on. "Instead, I'm going to concentrate on the endurance ride. There won't be anybody telling us what to do, so I should be okay."

"Great idea," Linda said enthusiastically. "You and Rocket are terrific on the trail. I wouldn't be surprised if you won."

Bob smiled at her. "So, since I'm practicing for trail rides, what do you say we get this one going? Or are you too humiliated after your last defeat?"

Linda grinned back as they joined Ronnie and got on their horses. If Bob felt good enough to start teasing her, he must be okay. She reached out and grabbed his hat. "You'll have to catch me if you want this back." Then they took off running.

They raced around the meadows down in the valley. Then Ronnie led the way up to a secret canyon in the mountainside where they rested, had a picnic dinner, and watered the horses. By the end of the day, they were happy but worn out. Bob said good night outside the stables.

Linda and Ronnie led their horses into their stalls. Ronnie quickly got her horse untacked and bedded down. Linda took her time. She knew she would dream of racing tonight.

"See you later, Linda," Ronnie called as she left.

Stifling a yawn, Linda stepped out of the stall. She was dead tired—so tired that she bumped into someone as she left the barn. It was Laurie Cavendish, entering the barn for her nightly check.

Linda didn't even think about it until the next morning. When she led Amber out of her stall, Linda noticed that her horse was limping. She lifted Amber's hoof and discovered a pinecone wedged between the horseshoe and the wall of the hoof. "You poor girl!" she said. She pulled out the cone, but Amber was still limping.

Linda put Amber back in her stall and went to find Hank. He came and inspected the hoof with a gentleness that he seldom showed to the campers.

"She flinches a little when I press the frog," he said, pointing to the triangular pad inside the hoof. "Any idea why that should be?"

"There was a pinecone wedged in her hoof," Linda said.

"When did you ride last?" Hank asked.

"Yesterday afternoon. My brother and I went on a trail ride," Linda said.

"Didn't you check her hooves after the ride?" Hank asked.

Linda tried to remember. She'd been awfully sleepy. She was sure she would have checked—she always did. And yet . . . "I don't know," she had to admit.

Hank let go of Amber's leg and straightened up. "Your horse can't be ridden today. We'll have to see about tomorrow."

Linda nodded glumly. Losing a day's practice would be a real setback, but it was more important that Amber's hoof get better.

Hank headed out of the stable, and then turned

back. "Oh, Craig?" he said. "That'll be ten demerits." Then he left.

Linda stared after him in dismay. She now had
twenty-five demerits—she was halfway to being disqualified for the final show!

7 ◆◆◆◆

Linda shook with anger. Would it be so terrible for Hank Harrington to give someone the benefit of the doubt? But that was the problem—doubt. If only she could be sure she'd checked Amber's hooves! What if she hadn't?

Linda buried her face in her horse's silky mane. "I'd never do anything to hurt you, Amber—you know that."

Amber nickered softly and gently pawed the ground.

"All right. I won't worry about you," Linda said gratefully. "But I promise I'll *always* check your hooves—no matter how tired I am."

Amber snorted and bobbed her head as if accepting the bargain. Linda gave the mare a good scratching before she led her outside to the small paddock.

As long as she was feeling rotten anyway, Linda

decided she would muck out Amber's stall. No sense spoiling a *good* day with that chore, she thought.

Linda got a pitchfork and wheelbarrow from behind the stable. Then she began lifting the soiled bedding out of the stall.

As she swung a forkful of straw toward the wheelbarrow, something in it caught her eyes. Something that didn't belong there. She dropped the straw on the floor of the stall and spread it out.

Linda stared in surprise. "How did this—?" she said out loud. Her eyes weren't playing tricks on her. It was a pinecone.

But she'd just thrown it away! Linda scooped up the pinecone and quickly walked over to the garbage can. There, inside, was the cone she had removed from Amber's hoof. So she wasn't going crazy.

Linda held up the newly discovered cone. As she looked at it, she saw that it was cracked in the middle. Several of its brittle branches had broken off.

No way did Amber pick up two pinecones in one trail ride, Linda thought. What if Amber didn't pick up that cone on the trail at all? Maybe it was in her bedding all along.

Using the pitchfork, Linda sifted through the straw bedding. No more pinecones. She paused for a moment, thinking. The straw for the bedding came in bales. Even if a pinecone did get mixed in with it, the baling process would have squashed it flat.

Linda's eyes darkened with anger. That left only one other way the pinecones could have gotten into the stall. Somebody had left them there—after deliberately wedging a pinecone into Amber's hoof!

It all made a horrible kind of sense. The first try hadn't worked—the pinecone had broken in the middle. So the person had just dropped it in the stall and used a second one.

It wasn't hard for Linda to put a face and a name on that person. Who else but Laurie Cavendish? Laurie had been entering the stable the night before as Linda was leaving.

Ever since Linda had come to camp, nasty things had been happening to her. Even though Laurie always pretended not to notice Linda, she'd been around whenever something bad had happened. Linda remembered the horse fight, the loosened cinch strap—and now Amber going lame. Each time, Laurie had been there.

Why was Laurie doing these things to her? Why did she hate her?

For a second, Linda thought about going to Hank Harrington. But what proof did she really have? A broken pinecone and a bunch of stories about his favorite rider. Hank would probably think she was making it all up to get out of the demerits he'd given her.

She couldn't even talk to Bob. He thought Laurie was about the best thing in camp.

"You missed breakfast, you know," a voice said from outside the stall. Linda turned to see Mary Ryan leaning against the door frame.

"I didn't feel hungry," Linda answered, energetically swinging her pitchfork.

"You're going to miss riding class—" Mary stopped when she saw Linda's eyes fill with tears. "What's the matter?"

"I won't be going," Linda told her. "Amber's gone lame—somebody tried to hurt her!" She showed Mary the pinecones, one from Amber's foot, the other from the hay.

Mary looked at them, wide-eyed but serious. Maybe it wasn't enough evidence to convince Hank Harrington, but Mary was impressed. Linda didn't tell her about suspecting Laurie. But she was sure now that it wasn't just her imagination—or just a case of practical jokes. Something unpleasant was going on. Linda was determined to find out what—and *why*.

"I've got to get moving," Mary told her. "See you later."

Charlie Vine walked in with a message from Tony Gordon. Since she couldn't ride, Linda was supposed to report to Vivian Scott at the crafts shack.

Linda spent the morning with Vivian, sorting out leather-working kits. It was quiet in the shack, and Linda spent a lot of time trying to figure out what to do about Laurie Cavendish.

By noontime, she still didn't have any ideas, but she was starving. A counselor stepped out onto the dining hall porch and rang the bell for lunch. Linda gave a broad grin. She certainly knew what to do now— make up for that lost breakfast!

That afternoon Linda took Amber to their care and grooming class. Amber had stopped favoring her hoof and showed no pain or tenderness. Tony Gordon examined the hoof and said Amber would be ready for riding by morning.

"That's good news about your horse," Mary Ryan said as the class broke up. "Are you coming to the sing-along after dinner?"

"Sure," Linda said with a smile. "I think Amber's had enough of me today."

There wasn't much singing at the sing-along, however. Instead, Tony Gordon told a creepy story about the Freak Snowstorm of '78, when a mountain blizzard caught four campers on the trail. Only three made it back. According to Tony, the ghost of the fourth frozen rider could sometimes be seen at night, moaning and scratching at the windows of the bunk-houses, trying to come in and get warm.

Tony was a good storyteller, and he brought his tale to a deliciously shuddery close. By then, the campfire had died down to a pile of embers. Linda noticed that some of the kids weren't so eager to head off into the darkness.

That night, Linda was the last person in her cabin to turn in. Unable to sleep, she lay in bed, listening to the steady breathing of the girls around her. Outside she could hear the wind scratching the leaves togeth-er in the treetops. She smiled. Just like the ghost from the story scratching at the window—she hoped Tony hadn't given anyone a nightmare.

An owl hooted, and Linda jumped. I hope he doesn't give *me* nightmares, she thought. She lay back and strained her ears, hoping to hear the distant howl of a coyote.

Instead, she heard another noise—a soft rustling sound, outside the window.

Linda sat up in bed, peering toward the window. Bright moonlight outside threw a pale glow on a figure in a long white gown, floating ghostlike past the cabin.

For a brief second, Linda thought about the lost rider. Then she grinned at herself. Probably Kate playing a little joke. In a second, she'd burst in, moaning, and scare everybody in the bunkhouse.

But the figure didn't head for the doorway to give the campers a scare. It silently kept moving. At the edge of the bunkhouse, the figure turned around for a moment, and Linda saw its face. Laurie Cavendish! What was she doing outside in the middle of the night?

Linda decided to follow her. If she was going to play another trick on Amber . . .

As swiftly and silently as she could, Linda got out of bed and pulled on a pair of tennis shoes and a robe. She held her breath as she tiptoed toward the door.

A board creaked underfoot, and Pam muttered in her sleep and rolled over. Linda forced herself to walk quietly, even though it made for slow going.

She opened the door and peeked out. Nobody! Maybe she'd been *too* slow.

Linda slipped outside, letting the door close with a soft click. She peered around. The moon and the stars provided some light, but it was still dark.

There was a noise as if pebbles were being scraped against one another. Linda moved silently toward the gravel path on her right.

There! Just ahead she was able to make out a ghostly white figure gliding along the path that led to the swimming hole. Her heart leapt. Even though she knew who it was, this whole situation had a spooky feel to it.

Linda stepped off the path and walked on the grass beside it. She didn't want to make any noise as she followed. She stayed close to the line of trees. If Laurie did turn around, Linda would be hard to spot.

All at once Linda shivered as the cool night breeze cut through her thin pajamas. She stopped for a second and looked over her shoulder at her cozy, warm cabin. Now she hoped she wouldn't hear a coyote howl!

Just ahead she could see a long finger of moonlight reflecting on still water. She had almost reached the swimming hole—and the end of the path.

Linda's heartbeat quickened.

As Laurie entered the clearing around the swimming hole, she stopped and stared out over the water. Linda continued to move closer, taking care to stay hidden in the shadow of the trees.

Laurie stood for a long time, as if hypnotized by the

water. Finally she moved again. She walked over to a large rock that the kids used for diving. Then she sank down onto the stone. The movement was so abrupt, it looked as if her legs had given way under her. She sat very still, her elbows resting on her knees, her back to Linda.

Then the silence was broken. Linda heard a muffled sound as Laurie lowered her head to her knees.

Linda wouldn't have believed her ears if she hadn't seen Laurie's shoulders shaking, too. Laurie Cavendish was sobbing.

8 ♦♦♦♦

Linda didn't know what to do. She wanted to rush over to Laurie and ask her what was wrong. But how could she explain what she was doing there?

And yet—Laurie was sobbing as though her heart would break. How could Linda just turn around and go back to the cabin as if nothing had happened?

Finally, Linda decided that that was all she *could* do. She ran back to her cabin, kicked off her tennis shoes, and climbed into bed. She was still cold, so she pulled the covers up around her, tucking them under her shoulders. Then she waited, listening.

After what seemed like hours, she heard footsteps on the gravel walkway outside. Laurie was heading back to her cabin. Then things were silent once more.

Linda lay awake for a long time, wondering about what she had seen and heard. Why had Laurie been crying? What did the camp's star rider have to cry about?

Whatever it was, it must have been pretty serious. Laurie had really fallen to pieces out on that rock. Just thinking about the scene made Linda feel sorry for her. Tomorrow morning, she decided, she'd break the ice—talk to Laurie while they were alone in the stable. Maybe what Laurie needed was a friend. Maybe Laurie had trouble at home. Or maybe—

Linda suddenly felt a cold chill, even under the warm covers. Maybe Laurie's problem was her conscience. Was she feeling guilty about the rotten things she had done?

Without any answers to her questions, Linda fell into a troubled sleep.

The next morning Linda woke up bleary-eyed. At first she couldn't understand why she felt so tired. Then she remembered the night before. For a moment she wondered if she had dreamed it.

There was no time to go to the stable before breakfast, so Linda went straight to the dining hall. She looked around for Laurie, and finally spotted her sitting next to Bob.

The two were talking quietly. There was, Linda

thought, a slight puffiness around Laurie's eyes. But other than that, there was no sign that anything had happened.

With a spoonful of cereal halfway to her mouth, Linda paused to yawn.

"The pace is finally getting to you, huh?" Mary Ryan leaned across the table with a teasing grin on her face.

Linda thought about telling Mary what had happened the night before. Then she decided she couldn't. She had intruded on Laurie's privacy. She had to keep what she had seen to herself.

Instead, Linda forced herself to grin back at Mary. "I wonder how many demerits you get if you fall asleep in the saddle?" she asked.

"Just remember that it's unsafe to yawn while posting at a trot." Mary imitated Hank Harrington perfectly.

Linda burst into a genuine laugh at Mary's impersonation. "I'll do my best to remember," she promised, rising from the table.

Luckily for Linda, that day's class covered something she could do in her sleep—practice for the barrel race. Everyone rode a lot more smoothly now than they had at the gymkhana, but she and Amber had been practicing, too.

When her turn came, Linda signaled Amber into a gallop and charged toward the barrels. "Go, Amber, go!" she whispered, leaning into the first turn. They came around the first barrel, edging perilously close to it, but never touching.

Then Linda shifted her weight, and they headed around the next barrel. Another shift, another barrel. Each passage brought them within a whisker's breadth of the barrels, but they never came any nearer—or lost their rhythm.

As she reined Amber in at the finish, Linda saw Tony Gordon look up from his watch. "Beautiful, Miss Craig. I've never seen anyone take the barrels so quickly. Take a bow."

Linda grinned as she realized that Tony was asking her to show off the trick she'd been practicing with Amber. Stretching out her foot, she nudged Amber behind the right leg with her toe.

Immediately, Amber extended her left leg and brought her right leg back, bending at the knees. She bowed her head till her nose almost touched the ground.

"A graceful bow. Congratulations. You can take the rest of the class off." Tony grinned at her. "Besides, I saw you yawning over on the sidelines."

Linda stifled another yawn as she led Amber from

the ring. "Thanks, girl," she whispered. "I feel sorry for the other kids. They don't have smart horses who can cover for them."

By lunchtime some of Linda's energy was starting to return. She looked forward to going swimming that afternoon. The cool water would clear the last of the cobwebs from her head.

It worked. The rest of the day went well, and Linda didn't have to worry about dozing off during that evening's Talent Night. She also found out why Mary had developed such a perfect Hank Harrington impersonation. She was in a skit, with Kate playing Tony Gordon and Janey in a fake beard as Stan O'Neill.

The next morning as she left the dining hall after breakfast, Linda heard someone calling her name.

Ronnie Ryberg came hurrying after her. "Just the person I wanted to see." Ronnie's voice was tight, her words coming out very fast.

Linda had figured out that Ronnie talked quickly when she was shy or nervous. She hadn't heard Ronnie speak this fast since the first couple of days at camp.

Ronnie leaned close to Linda and crooked her forefinger, gesturing for Linda to bend toward her.

"There's an important Crystal Valley Ranch tradition occurring this evening," Ronnie whispered. "Fudge Friday."

Linda straightened up. "Huh?" She thought she must have misunderstood. "I thought this was Wednesday."

Ronnie shrugged. "So, no tradition is perfect," she said. "Anyway, be in the kitchen at nine o'clock tonight. Knock twice and say Ronnie sent you. But don't tell anyone. Okay?"

Before Linda could even nod, Ronnie had darted off.

For the rest of the day, through her horsemanship classes, swimming period, and dinner, Linda wondered what was going on. Finally evening came—an "individual choice" evening without an organized activity. Linda had been planning to spend her time in the crafts shack, finishing a wallet for Bronco. Now a new adventure beckoned.

At two minutes to nine, Linda set off for the dining hall, trying to look casual. She shoved her hands in the back pockets of her jeans and strolled along, whistling.

Along the way she met Mary Ryan and Ellen Lake, who was also in her riding group. Both girls were also strolling and whistling.

As soon as she saw the two of them, Linda began to giggle. "Guess we don't look too casual, huh?"

They walked the rest of the way together and tiptoed into the darkened dining hall.

"Do you know what this is about?" Linda whispered.

"I heard rumors last year," Mary said. "Now I'm finally going to find out." She knocked twice on the kitchen door.

"Who's there?" came the rapid reply.

"Ronnie sent us," the three girls chorused in whispers.

"Enter," said the voice. The door swung open.

The three girls walked through the doorway into a shadowy, dark kitchen illuminated only by the rays of four flashlights. Even so, the conspirators had covered the outside windows with old blankets.

"Welcome to Fudge Friday," Ronnie said in a loud whisper. "This is the night we raid the supplies and whip up a batch of gooey, chocolaty, scrumptious fudge."

"Sounds delicious," said Mary.

Ronnie immediately put a hand over Mary's mouth. "All we have to do is keep from getting caught by the cook, who would chase us out of here with her rolling pin." Ronnie's eyes sparkled with laughter.

The other girls looked at each other, and began grinning.

"Now, let's get to work." Ronnie rolled up her sleeves. The other kids did the same.

While Linda, Mary, and a girl named Karen started assembling the supplies, more Desperados kept arriving. Pam, Janey, and Kate all joined them. Then Fran came sneaking in. A lot of High Riders were already there, and even some Colts turned up. Soon the kitchen was wall-to-wall bodies.

"How many people did you invite, Ronnie?" Linda asked.

"I wanted to make sure we had enough," she replied.

"Well, I think you overdid it."

Kids were constantly bumping into one another. Elbows got jostled. Butter, sugar, and chocolate went flying.

Despite Ronnie's constant reminders to be quiet, pans clattered and cupboard doors banged. Each loud noise was followed by a chorus of "Shhhhhhhhhhh!" followed by long bursts of giggling.

"I can hardly wait to taste the fudge, after all the *wholesome* food," Karen said, buttering a pan.

"I think the food here is good," Mary said.

"Oh, it is," Karen agreed. "But it isn't *fudge.*" She

growled the last word as she squinted her blue eyes and patted her stomach.

Giggles escaped from Mary and Linda, which brought another round of shushes from the other campers.

"I hope we don't get caught," Linda whispered. "I have so many demerits I'd miss the final competition."

"I wouldn't worry about it," one of the High Riders whispered back. "This is my third year here, and my third Fudge Friday. I haven't been caught yet."

Linda relaxed, getting down to work simmering the delicious-smelling concoction over low heat.

After what seemed like hours, Ronnie pronounced the thick, dark goo ready to pour into the pans. Then she set these into dishpans filled with ice water. "Instant cool—" she started to say.

"What's that?" Mary asked, interrupting her.

"What's what?" Ronnie replied. Then her eyebrows went up, and her finger flew to her lips. "Shhhhh!" She had heard it, too. "Be quiet, everyone."

They all listened, hearts pounding, knees turning to jelly. Very distinctly now they heard a *plop, squeak—plop, squeak.* Someone wearing sneakers was walking across the dining hall and heading for the kitchen door.

"Take everything and head for the pantry. Go!" was Ronnie's whispered order.

After grabbing everything they could, the kids dove into the pantry. It was only large enough for about six people. Somehow, more than twenty kids crammed themselves inside.

Ronnie was the last in, switching off her flashlight and elbowing into the crowd while balancing the last pan of fudge.

She closed the door just as the rubber soles started to squeak across the waxed linoleum of the kitchen floor.

Around the entire pantry door they saw a halo of light. The person out there must have turned the kitchen light on.

"Who's there?" a woman's deep voice called out.

"Uh-oh!" Ronnie whispered.

All the campers tried to hold their laughter in, but one at a time they lost control and began laughing out loud.

"I said, who's there?" the woman repeated.

Now they heard the rubber soles squeaking right up to the pantry door. "All right, come on out."

Slowly Ronnie inched the door open and poked her head out. "Um, hi there, Mrs. Thompson," she said with a big grin on her face.

"'Hi there, Mrs. Thompson.' What kind of a greeting is that? It's ten o'clock at night, kiddo. You're in my kitchen, and you say, 'Hi there, Mrs. Thompson'?"

"I'm sorry. I really am. And I take complete responsibility for this. I really do," Ronnie said all in one breath.

"So, you didn't have any help at all making that fudge I smell?" Mrs. Thompson asked.

"Fudge?" Ronnie asked innocently.

"Don't try that act on me," the large, white-haired woman boomed. "This place positively reeks of fudge." She glared in the doorway. "The rest of you had better come out of there—and bring that pan with you."

One at a time, like clowns piling out of a tiny circus car, the campers came tumbling out of the pantry.

"Twenty-one? There were *twenty-one* of you in my pantry?"

Silently they nodded.

"Well, I'll just have to see if twenty-one campers make better fudge than one terrific cook—namely me. Come on and let me taste that fudge."

"It's not quite hard yet," Linda answered.

"Haven't you ever heard of spoons? Ronnie, run over to that drawer and dig out twenty-two spoons. I've been trying to catch you in the act for five years—the least I can get is a taste of this fudge."

Ronnie stared, stricken. "Y-you knew all along?" she faltered.

"Uh-huh. I'd have to be blind not to know. The next morning, my kitchen looks like it was invaded by an army." Mrs. Thompson looked at all the girls. "And now I know why. Well, let's see if the clean-up is worth it." And she took her spoon and dug it into the still soft fudge.

"Well?" Mary asked.

Mrs. Thompson rolled the sweet bite around in her mouth, swallowed, and then she answered, "This is the best fudge I have ever tasted."

They all cheered.

"And I hope that you remember to invite me to Fudge Friday from now on!"

The entire group sat on the floor around Mrs. Thompson and dug into the best chocolate fudge *any* of them had ever eaten.

Despite her short night's sleep on Fudge Friday,

Linda had no trouble waking up early the next morning.

Amber nickered softly as Linda drew back the bolt on her stall and went in to stroke her.

As she slipped Amber's halter on, Linda said, "The kids and I had a great time last night. We had some wonderful fudge, too. I'm sorry I had to leave you with just a rack of hay."

Linda glanced over at the rack and stopped. The rack was still full. It didn't look as though Amber had even touched it. That wasn't like her.

Linda tugged at her horse's halter, directing her attention to her food. "Come on, Amber. Don't you want to eat?" But Amber stepped back and held her head down. No amount of coaxing could interest her in the hay rack.

Linda felt a sinking feeling. Not eating was a bad sign. Reluctantly, she went to find Hank Harrington.

Hank dropped what he was doing and came straight back with Linda to inspect the palomino. "She looks healthy enough," he said, sounding puzzled. "To be safe, sit out this morning's practice. If she isn't better by noon, we'll send for the vet."

Linda blinked back her tears. She was surprised

when Hank patted her shoulder just before he slipped out of the stall. But it didn't make her feel any better.

"Please don't be sick, Amber," she pleaded, stroking the silky golden neck.

Amber responded with a nuzzle. The nuzzling soon turned into an insistent nudge. "What is it, girl?" Linda asked. "What do you want?"

Amber nudged her again, right in the front pocket of her blue jeans. This was where Linda always kept Amber's treats.

"Oh, so you want a treat, do you?" Linda asked, smiling as Amber gave her a look. Then she paused suddenly, stared at the horse, and said, "Wait a minute—why are you begging for treats if you're off your feed?"

Linda ran to get a bucketful of grain and brought it back to Amber. The horse started to eat it eagerly.

"You're not off your feed at all!" Linda exclaimed. She looked up at the wall rack. "So what have you got against this hay?"

Linda walked to the rack, leading Amber. The horse whinnied and pawed the ground frantically. She didn't want to go near the rack. She wanted out of the stall—right now!

"Shhh. Calm down, girl," Linda said in a soothing

tone. She attached Amber's lead rope to the halter and led her out of the stall.

Linda went back in and stood directly in front of the rack. She sniffed the air, catching a sharp stink that didn't belong with the barn smells. The closer she came to the rack, the more acrid the smell became. Linda began digging through the hay, scooping up handfuls and throwing them on the ground.

With only a couple more handfuls to go, Linda touched something that shouldn't have been in the rack.

Slowly she pulled out a long strip of cloth, coughing from the sharp fumes that wafted from it.

No wonder Amber hadn't wanted to go near this thing, she thought.

Someone had soaked it in liniment!

9 ◆◆◆◆

Linda gathered up all the old hay in the stall and tossed the fouled stuff outside on the trash heap. She brought in fresh hay, led Amber in, and was standing outside the stall watching the palomino eat when Ronnie rushed up to her. "Linda, I just heard that Amber's off her feed."

Ronnie peeked over the top board into the stall. Then she turned back to Linda. Her eyebrows were raised and she looked surprised. "I guess I heard wrong."

"Somebody was trying to make it *look* like she's off her feed," Linda said angrily. She ran over to the trash barrel where she'd thrown the liniment-soaked rag. Pulling it out, she showed it to Ronnie. "This was in Amber's hay rack," she said.

"Who'd do something like that?" Ronnie demanded.

"I don't know," Linda said. "But I do know that I'm getting really tired of all this stupid stuff going on around here."

"What do you mean?"

"This," she said, shaking the rag, "is only the latest thing that's happened. The other day there were two pinecones in the bedding—one of them somehow got wedged in Amber's hoof. And there was my loosened girth strap at the gymkhana."

"It was loosened?" Ronnie said in shock. She thought for a moment, then took the rag from Linda. "I'm going to tell Hank what's going on."

Linda became nervous. "Do we have to?" she asked.

"We do," Ronnie replied firmly. "Something even more serious could happen, unless we tell him."

"I don't know. It seems that, well, whenever I talk to Hank about anything, I always wind up getting demerits."

"That won't happen this time," Ronnie said. "Trust me." She marched out of the stable.

Linda stood talking quietly to Amber until Hank and Ronnie came in. Ronnie looked strained. Hank Harrington looked angry.

Linda braced herself for hard questions from Hank, but there were none. There was almost no conversation. He had Ronnie fetch some grain in a plastic pail, and he watched as Amber eagerly ate it.

"She's fine, all right," he said. "Let her digest for an hour. She'll be ready for the trail ride today."

This was the last day of lessons. In the afternoon, the counselors were taking the campers along the route of Saturday's trail-riding competition. The riders and their mounts would spend Friday resting up for the big event.

The campers all saddled up after lunch. For most of them, this would be an easygoing ride in the country. The real competitors, like Bob, would be scouting the route carefully, checking out every possibility to pull ahead on the course. Linda silently wished Bob good luck. The trail competition would be his big chance for a win.

The afternoon sun was bright, but the wind was brisker than usual. Most of the kids wore windbreakers or hooded sweatshirts as they rode.

Linda couldn't believe how all the Desperados had improved in their riding. Mary, who had always kidded around, looked much more serious and proud as she rode Red. Young Ellen Lake did a much better job of controlling her horse, Wonder.

"I wonder if *we* look different, too," Linda said as she patted Amber.

Amber snorted, as if asking Linda how they could get better than they already were.

As they rode along the trail, Linda noticed that the weather seemed to be changing. She stopped and looked up at the sky. Clouds had appeared, looking heavy and wet as if they were filled with snow.

"Silly," she said out loud to herself. "It's still summer." But she was glad that she had remembered to bring her light jacket.

She shivered as Ronnie led the way through a stream, some of the riders getting splashed with icy water. The wind was picking up, too.

Linda felt inside her jacket. She'd wrapped a blueberry muffin in a napkin and stuck it and an apple into her pocket. A little high-energy snack would be welcome in this sudden chill, but she thought she'd save it for a little later.

They continued on to the top of a ridge, and Linda was surprised to find that the weather had grown even colder. She shivered as a sudden chill ran across her skin. It wasn't just from the cold. Linda was beginning to feel a little worried.

Ellen Lake began talking nervously, looking up at the lowering skies. "You know, Tony Gordon's snow-storm story wasn't all make-believe. Freak snowstorms sometimes roll in without any warning this time of the year." She looked back along the trail. "And we've got a long ride back to camp."

Gooseflesh rose on Linda's arms, and she hunched her shoulders. The sagebrush had turned a leaden gray, with a dank wind tearing through it.

Then, almost on cue, fat snowflakes began falling on them.

"I don't believe this," Linda said, pulling up the hood of her jacket.

She was beginning to get frightened. Even a small snow squall could be dangerous on these mountain trails—especially for the younger kids.

Hank Harrington came riding back from the head of the group. "We're turning back—now. We're just lucky we didn't get up to the harder part of the trail. This is going to be the checkpoint, where we make sure everyone is on their way back. Nancy Bauer will take over. Till she gets here, Ronnie, you're in charge. Pick someone to stay with you."

Ellen looked scared, and neither Mary nor the other girls seemed too eager.

"I've got a hood, and my jacket is probably the warmest," Linda said. "If you like, I'll stay."

"Great, Linda." Ronnie smiled.

Hank gave a curt nod and led the rest of the group down the trail.

Amber didn't like standing out in the wet snow. She kept stamping and turning her back to the wind. Linda kept turning her around so she could see who was coming back down the trail.

The last of the Desperados had passed them now, heading for camp. Tony Gordon reined in beside Ronnie and Linda. "Why are you sticking around?" he asked.

"We're supposed to wait here for Nancy Bauer," Ronnie said, "to make sure all the kids are heading back."

"You'd think this snow would be a clue," Tony said. "Well, she can't be too far away." He rode on.

By now, groups of High Riders were passing by. Linda eagerly looked for Bob, but he wasn't with any of the other kids.

The wind began to sting Linda's face, and she had to squint her eyes to see. Her brother still hadn't turned up. Linda began shivering, and it wasn't all from the cold.

A small knot of riders came by, but no Nancy Bauer, no Laurie Cavendish—and no Bob Craig.

"Ronnie . . ." Linda began, feeling really scared.

"It's probably just a flurry," Ronnie said, trying to make Linda feel better. "Maybe Bob is with Nancy."

They heard a horse making its way through the gathering gloom. Nancy Bauer rode up, her face tight. "We're missing two people," she said. "A C.I.T. and—"

"And my brother," Linda finished. "What are we going to do?"

"You people are going back," Nancy said. "Hank will have to organize the counselors into a search party. I'll stay here, in case they come heading back."

Even as she said this, they heard another rider approaching. Linda could hardly see into the distance, but she recognized the long auburn hair of Laurie Cavendish.

Linda urged Amber forward. "Where's my brother?" she asked anxiously.

Laurie pointed up the trail. "Trouble," she said. "I think—"

"Listen!" Linda cut her off.

They all stared through the curtain of falling snow, hearing hoofbeats but unable to see the horse racing straight for them.

"It must be Rocket," Linda said. "But Bob's riding him too fast for this weather!"

Linda jumped off Amber as the other three rose up in their stirrups, trying to make out the horse and rider. Finally, with a sick feeling, Linda saw that Bob wasn't riding him at all.

Rocket's saddle was empty!

— 10 ••••

The frightened, riderless horse came galloping up but shied to a halt when he saw Linda. She grabbed for the reins dangling near the ground, but Rocket was thoroughly spooked. He skittered away, eyes wide with fear.

Linda was shocked as she looked at the bay horse. His mouth was rimmed with foam, and the whites of his eyes showed.

He had obviously come a long way without a rider to guide him. This and the howl of the wind were enough to put him into this wild panic.

"Hey, Rocket, you know me," Linda said softly, moving slowly toward him. "Calm down, fella. We've got to find Bob."

Rocket sidestepped away from her, his head going down. At least he didn't run away. He knew that

Linda was a friend, even if he was reluctant to come too near.

"Rocket—" Laurie called out.

The horse's head swung around toward Linda, and she was able to get hold of his bridle. "Take it easy now," she said, gently stroking his neck.

"What happened up there?" Nancy asked.

"Bob and I wound up in the lead—he's really a good trail rider," Laurie explained. "Before we realized it, we'd pulled way ahead. He handled the gate and the cavalletti jumps, and I guess . . ." She hesitated, looking at Linda. "I guess he got overconfident. He rode on ahead of me. Then the snow started, and he didn't come back."

"Can you lead me to where you last saw him?" Linda asked, then turned to the others. "I've got to go after Bob."

Nancy Bauer frowned. "You can't do that," she said. "It's too dangerous."

"Bob is my brother," Linda stated simply. "If he's really in trouble up there, he may need help right away."

Laurie spoke up. "I'll go with her," she volunteered.

"Ronnie, take Rocket's reins," Nancy ordered. She slipped a pair of saddlebags off her horse and held them out to Linda. "There's a flashlight, a first-aid kit, and a few other things you might need."

Linda slung the bags over Amber's shoulders. Nancy went on, "Ronnie and I will catch up with Hank and get you some help." She leaned forward. "I don't think I need to tell you to be careful," she said. "But I will, anyway."

"Thanks," Linda said gratefully. She turned to Laurie, who had already turned Lady Jane back into the wind.

As they set off up the trail, Linda thought for the first time about what a chance she was taking. She also wondered if she had done the right thing in letting Laurie come along.

But I didn't let her come along, she corrected herself. She wanted to come. Why all of a sudden did she have this great interest in Bob Craig's safety? As far as Linda knew, Laurie had never shown the slightest concern for anyone.

Then, all at once, Linda knew what was bothering her. She had always thought Laurie might be behind all of the weird stuff that had happened to her. Now Bob was missing—*after* he had ridden ahead with Laurie. And Linda was blindly following Laurie up the same trail!

I don't even know that this is the route they took,

Linda thought. I have only Laurie's word that she and Bob came this way.

She turned and looked over her shoulder. The snow was coming down like mad, and she could see no light from the camp. Going back alone could be dangerous, perhaps as dangerous as going on with Laurie. If she did turn back, what would happen to Bob? Linda gritted her teeth and forced herself not to think about Laurie. I have to keep going, she told herself, I *have* to.

The trail wasn't easy—especially with the trail-riding obstacles in the way—and the horses couldn't make much speed, fighting their way against the wind. After what seemed like forever, Linda heard Laurie yelling to her. The wind tore away most of her words, but Linda understood that this was where Laurie had turned back that afternoon.

Linda rode up next to Laurie, looking at the ground. Of course, the snow had covered over any tracks that had been there. Together, they moved forward, trying to get any speed they could out of the horses.

Ahead of them appeared another obstacle—a chest-high stone wall. Linda pulled Amber back, ready to urge her to jump. She clucked to Amber and touched the horse's sides with her heels. But Amber refused to budge.

"Come on, girl, this is important," Linda begged. Amber dug in her front hooves, and pricked up her ears. Linda listened, too. Above the wind, Linda thought she heard a very faint voice floating toward her.

"Hello? Hello? Is somebody there?"

"Bob!" Linda yelled. "Bob, it's me! Where are you? Keep talking." She brought Amber closer to the wall and dug out the flashlight. Standing in the stirrups, she shone the light over the wall.

On the other side was a pile of stones, half-buried in drifting snow. Then part of the pile moved—Bob!

Linda kicked her feet free of the stirrups and got ready to jump over the wall, but Laurie grabbed her arm. "Careful," she said. "It's a dry-stone wall—nothing's cemented together."

Even sliding cautiously over the wall, Linda brought down a shower of stones. However, with Laurie's warning, she didn't bring them down on Bob. "Are you all right?" she asked, kneeling beside him.

"Cold. But I'll be fine now." Bob managed a grin, even though he was shivering convulsively.

"Can you move?"

"No. My foot's caught. Rocket got spooked and refused the jump. He sent *me* over, though. Then Rocket bumped into the wall and knocked part of it down on me." He brushed some snow off the pile of stones that held him prisoner. "I managed to get some off, but—"

"They're too heavy for you," Linda finished. "Well, we're here now." She looked in concern at the way his leg twisted as it disappeared into the pile. "Does it hurt?"

"It doesn't hurt as long as I don't move," Bob said, "so I don't think it's broken. I just can't get it out."

Laurie came sliding over the wall. "Maybe we can move the rocks away."

Linda had forgotten that Laurie was there. She turned, startled, then looked back at the pile. "Some of those rocks are pretty huge," she said. "I don't think we can budge them."

Laurie strained to lift one of the bigger rocks, with no success. Then she sat down, propping her feet against it, and shoved, using her legs for leverage. The stone rocked a little, but that was the only effect. "You're right," she said.

Linda shoved her hands into the pockets of her jacket and discovered the apple and blueberry muffin she had put there at lunch. "I don't suppose you're hungry?" she said, handing them to Bob.

"Starved is more like it." He took a big bite of muffin, swallowed, then chomped deeply into the apple.

Linda was already climbing back over the wall. She returned a moment later, bringing Nancy Bauer's saddlebags. "We've got some stuff to help you," she said, taking out the first-aid kit and a blanket, which she tucked around Bob. "But we've really got to get you out of here."

"Help's on the way," Laurie reminded her.

"We don't have time. This storm is getting worse." All at once the wind veered around, and Linda felt the sting of snowflakes being driven into her face. She looked up and turned on her flashlight. Flashing bits of snow danced in its beam.

"What would you suggest?" Bob asked. "I don't know what we can do."

But Linda *did* know what to do. "We forgot something," she said. "We've got more help right here."

Amber and Lady Jane had been standing with their backs to the storm. Now, as the wind changed, both of their heads appeared over the stone wall.

Linda dug into the saddlebags. Just as she hoped, it contained an extra length of lead rope. It might not work, she thought, but it was worth a try.

She put the flashlight in Bob's hands. "Turn this on, and hold it," she told him. "We're going to take a shot at moving some of these rocks."

Climbing back over the wall, she turned Amber around to face the wind. Her horse snorted but stood still while Linda tied a loop of rope over the saddle-horn. She tossed the rest over the wall.

"Wrap it around the biggest rock you can find," she called to Laurie.

"Ready!" Laurie yelled a moment later.

"Pull, Amber! Pull, girl," Linda said.

Amber took one step and then another. The rope was now pulled tight. In the feeble glow of the flashlight, Linda looked at her horse. Amber's breath, white in the chill air, was blasting out of her nostrils as she strained against the weight.

"It moved!" Bob shouted. "Another inch and it'll go over!" Amber snorted and lowered her head.

"Pull, Amber! Come on, girl," Linda said again. Slowly the horse shifted first one hoof, and then another. She planted them solidly into the rocks and dirt and pulled once again.

"That's it!" Bob yelled over the rattle of falling stones. "We're halfway there!"

Laurie managed to move some of the smaller stones, with Bob's help. Soon only one huge rock kept Bob pinned. They set the rope again, and once more Amber strained.

"Just a little more, girl. *Please,*" Linda urged.

At last, the stone shifted, and Laurie helped Bob scuttle backward—he was free!

Linda let Amber back up, and the big rock creaked back into position. Then she swarmed over the wall. Bob was already trying to stand up, groaning as pain shot through his stiff foot and ankle.

"Can you ride?" Laurie asked.

Bob winced as he rubbed his ankle. "I think so."

"We've got to try to get down off the mountain before this storm gets any worse," Linda said.

She and Laurie helped Bob up into Amber's saddle. Then, as Laurie mounted Lady Jane, Linda grabbed a handful of Amber's silky mane in her left hand. "Let's go, girl," she said, and began leading the horse back down the mountainside.

The snow was wet and heavy, coming down more like snowballs than flakes. In open places, the trail was beginning to glaze over with a thin, icy crust. The snow was drifting, hiding ruts and holes in the path. Amber could easily slip and fall.

Linda wondered how long it would take for help to arrive. It had better come quickly—she was starting to tire, and she could feel Bob reeling in the saddle above her.

Her own foot skidded on the ice. Crystal Valley was a good name for this place, she decided. When it snowed, the trails were like glass.

The bitter wind just wouldn't let up. It cut through her thin jacket and seemed to steer snowflakes straight for her eyes. But one glance up at Bob huddled in the saddle, the blanket wrapped around him, reminded her that there was someone in worse trouble.

They continued on, into the teeth of the wind. Linda's feet hurt from the cold. And her riding gloves didn't really keep the cold away, either. She was half-leaning against Amber now, stumbling along.

Then, ahead, they saw lights. Four figures came riding toward them—Hank Harrington, Nancy Bauer, Tony Gordon, and Stan O'Neill.

"Are we glad to see you!" Stan said.

Hank, all business, helped Bob down from Amber and onto the spare horse he'd been leading. Exhausted, Linda climbed onto Amber.

She was too tired to keep up with the others and fell behind. Laurie dropped back to stay with her.

"You were really terrific!" Laurie said. "Shifting those rocks and setting him free saved a lot of time. Bob owes you a lot."

"He owes you a lot, too," Linda said quietly.

Laurie shook her head. "I think we're just about even," she replied. "He listened to me a few times when I was down in the dumps. I told him how much I hate Crystal Valley."

"You hate Crystal Valley?" Linda asked, surprised.

"No," Laurie said quickly. "That's not true. I don't hate the ranch. What I hate is competitive riding. And that's what Crystal Valley is all about."

"But you're such a wonderful rider!" Linda exclaimed.

"I love working with horses and helping people ride better. But I hate riding in front of an audience full of people waiting to pounce on any mistake."

Linda remembered the night she had followed Laurie out to the swimming hole and heard her sobbing. She couldn't imagine herself feeling that bad about something like riding. "Then why do you keep coming here?" she asked.

"My parents make me," Laurie replied. "They still have fantasies about me making the Olympic equestrian team. I come to Crystal Valley because Hank knows how I feel and he doesn't push me." She grinned. "He even pretends not to see when I do a little teaching."

"You mean—"

"I mean Hank is nice to me only because he's given up on me," Laurie said.

Linda was amazed. It just proves that things aren't always what they seem, she thought.

"And . . . look, I owe you an apology," Laurie said. "You were right about Lady Jane starting the fight with Amber. When she's in a bad mood, she snaps." Laurie gave Linda a half-smile. "Almost as much as I do. I was feeling rotten about being at camp, and I gave you a real hard time. When I got friendly with your brother, he told me you were really okay. But by then it just got harder and harder to say anything to you."

"I thought I'd done something to make you hate me," Linda responded.

"Oh, no. It was all my fault. I really should have tried to be friendlier."

Linda and Laurie rode on in snowy silence, staring ahead, each thinking her own thoughts.

Laurie wasn't the one behind the nasty tricks on

Linda and Amber—Linda was sure of that now. But if it wasn't Laurie, then who was it—and why?

"I hope Bob will be able to ride by Saturday," Laurie said.

Linda grinned at her. "If I know my brother, he'll ride."

"Rocket should be fit, anyway. I told Ronnie to race back to the stable and get him cooled off and bedded down," Laurie said.

"Race," Linda muttered. Then came the odd sense of everything fitting into place. She sat up so abruptly in the saddle that Amber took it as a signal to stop.

"Now I know what it is," she said. "And I know who's been giving me all that trouble!"

11 ♦♦♦♦

The snow-covered little band rode into camp to find Hank and Ronnie waiting for them in Filly Alley. Cold and tired, Linda swung down off Amber, looked straight at Ronnie, and said, "Okay, Ronnie. Want to tell me why?"

Ronnie appeared scared for a second. Then defiantly she asked, "Why what?"

Linda took a deep breath. She almost wished she had never begun, but now she had to finish. "Why have you been trying to ruin my stay at camp? You loosened the girth on my saddle. You wedged the pinecone into Amber's hoof and hid that liniment-soaked rag in her hay rack. What made you do all that?"

Ronnie glanced up at Hank. "I didn't do anything," she said, her chin thrust out.

Hank looked from her to Linda in disbelief.

Linda kept staring at Ronnie. "You knew that Laurie and I didn't get along. So you kept setting up trouble, hoping that I'd blame Laurie and get her in trouble."

"I didn't—it's not—" All at once the energy seemed to drain from Ronnie, and she nodded her head. "I did it," she whispered. "All the stuff you said."

She shook her head as if she couldn't believe she *had* done those things. "I've watched Laurie get special treatment for the past five years, and I couldn't take it anymore. She doesn't even try, and she *still* wins awards."

Even in making a confession, Ronnie's eyes flashed with competitiveness. Linda remembered how deeply Ronnie had gotten into the race in the meadow—to the point of "forgetting" to warn Linda about the fence.

Ronnie's shoulders sagged again. "I decided to pull a trick on you, Linda, and get you to suspect Laurie. You'd complain to Hank, and she'd get in trouble.

"Loosening your cinch strap was going too far, though. I didn't think you'd be going that fast. . . ." Her words trailed off as she realized just how dangerous that trick had been.

When Ronnie spoke again, her eyes were wet with tears. "But you never told on Laurie once, Linda. You always took the blame yourself."

"I *suspected* Laurie and was furious at her," Linda admitted. "But I really couldn't say for sure that I had checked the girth or Amber's hooves. And I didn't have any proof that Laurie put the rag in Amber's hay rack. How could I blame her?"

"You really think I have it made, don't you?" Laurie said to Ronnie, speaking for the first time. "Ever since our first year at camp, you've been jealous of me, and I don't know why. You're the one who's going to ride in the Olympics someday. Not me. Don't you see? Hank criticizes your performance because he knows you can be the best. He doesn't bother with me because he knows I'm not going anywhere."

Hank stared at both girls, shaking his head. "My two best riders," he said. "And my two worst mistakes."

Ronnie shoved her hands into her pockets. She sniffed once and looked away. Her shoulders were hunched up, and her neck disappeared into the collar of her jacket.

They all stood silently, lost in their own thoughts.

Finally Ronnie asked Linda, "Tell me—when did you figure it all out?"

"On the ride back to camp," Linda explained. "It all fell into place. Laurie had just gone all-out to help Bob and me. I couldn't fit that with the person who had made my life miserable. So who was left? Then Laurie mentioned your name and the word 'race' together, and I thought back to the trail ride we took."

She sighed. "I also realized a few more things. You'd been around when I left Amber alone before the barrel race. You're good with horses. You could have gotten Amber to stand still while you wedged a pinecone into her hoof. You wandered into the stable soon after I found the liniment rag. I guess you needed it to show to Hank.

"The only thing I didn't figure out was why you'd done those things. Now I understand."

"I'm sorry," Ronnie said. Her tears spilled over, and she buried her face in her hands, crying.

Hank walked with her down to the end of the stable where they could be alone.

All at once Linda felt exhausted. "I don't know about you," she said to Laurie. "But all I can think of is going to bed."

"Me, too," Laurie admitted. "This has been one long day."

"I'm too tired and too angry to talk about this any more tonight," Hank was saying to Ronnie. "Come on, we have horses to bed down."

"First a special treat and then we put you to bed, Amber." Linda stroked her horse, then yawned. "After that, it's my turn."

Linda was allowed to sleep in the next morning. When she got up, she stared out the window in amazement. The sun was out, and the snow had all but disappeared.

Mountain weather sure can change fast, thought Linda. She quickly dressed and headed for the stables.

"Hello, sleepyhead," she heard a voice calling.

Linda turned to see Bob come riding past. Both he and Rocket looked good in spite of their ordeal.

"We've got some unfinished business up on that trail," Bob told his sister. "Scouting out the rest of the competition route."

"You're sure we won't get more snow today?" Linda asked, grinning.

"I don't know about snow," Bob answered. "But I bet we'll find lots of mud."

The mud was still there on Saturday, and Bob was wearing a lot of it when he and Rocket crossed the finish line for the trail-ride competition. But he was grinning in triumph, too. When the scores were posted, Bob Craig and Rocket were winners—their names were at the top of the list!

I'm so glad he won, Linda thought. He'd been feeling like a loser, and now he was a winner again.

Then Linda started thinking about her own troubles at camp. She wondered about Ronnie. The girl hadn't been around on Friday, and she hadn't ridden out on Saturday, either.

Linda hoped that Hank hadn't fired her. What she'd done was terribly wrong. But Linda figured that if *she* could forgive Ronnie, then Hank should. The problem was Hank didn't seem like the understanding type.

Sunday morning Bob and Linda were outside waiting for Doña and Bronco at the same spot where they had said good-bye two weeks earlier. When their grandparents finally arrived, Linda barely had time to hug each of them before she headed off to saddle Amber. Bob escorted Doña and Bronco to the arena.

Linda was surprised to see Laurie and Ronnie talking excitedly in front of Lady Jane's stall. She paused just inside the door, feeling awkward. When the two girls saw her, they ran up and hugged her. Both of their faces were beaming.

"Hey, Linda! We have great news," Laurie said as they walked to Amber's stall. "Hank talked to us this morning. He said he decided he might have treated us both unfairly. He's going to talk to my parents about competitive riding and me. If everything works out, I'll be coming to camp as an instructor."

"And I'm not going to be on the staff anymore," Ronnie said.

Linda didn't understand why Ronnie sounded so happy until she added, "Hank's been thinking of setting up a special training group—with hand-picked riders and even tougher practice. We'll probably be breaking our necks all summer, but we'll be riding. And, uh, let's face it, I was never very good as a counselor."

Linda let out a sigh. "I'm so glad! When I didn't see you the last couple of days, I—"

"I know," Ronnie said, so that Linda didn't have to finish the sentence. "You thought I was done for. Well, so did I. Hank didn't speak to me until this morning. First he laid on the demerits—surprise, surprise, I won't be competing today." She grimaced. "I deserved it, though. What I did was awful. And I really am sorry." She paused for a second. "Do you forgive me?"

"Apology accepted," Linda said. "Just send me an autographed picture—when you win your Olympic medal!"

Linda went into Amber's stall. The mare started nickering when she saw Linda. "Uh-oh, someone is raring to compete. Well, come on, girl. You and I have a date with some barrels."

Linda led Amber to the arena. After carefully checking her girth, she swung onto Amber's back, clucked to her, and headed out.

In the arena, Charlie Vine was tackling the barrels, cutting around them at high speed. He was followed by Ellen Lake, who took the course confidently. Next was Mary Ryan, who seemed a blur as she and Red raced smoothly to a finish.

Then it was Linda's turn. Shift, turn, shift, turn, Linda thought. She and Amber seemed to become one creature as they pounded around the barrels. They whipped their way along, and when they halted in front of the judges' stand, Tony Gordon nodded approvingly.

Linda let Amber take a bow.

Even before she heard her time, she knew it was the best she'd ever done. But when Hank Harrington as head judge made the announcement, she learned she'd ridden two-tenths of a second faster than any of the Desperados.

"First place," Linda exclaimed to Amber, who strutted in a circle with her knees high. "Good girl!"

After all the ribbons had been handed out, the final award of the day—the Crystal Valley Ranch Challenge Cup—was presented. It was a large silver-plated trophy and was awarded to the rider who had given the best performance during the whole camping season.

Hank held the trophy high over his head. It caught the light, shining long beams into the eyes of the audience.

He's letting the excitement build, Linda thought as

she joined her family in the stands. She reached out and gave Doña a giant hug.

"This year's winner of the Crystal Valley Ranch Challenge Cup is—Laurie Cavendish!" Hank shouted.

Laurie's mouth dropped open when she heard the announcement. Her pretty face was bright pink, and her cheeks were wet with tears.

Linda glanced over at Ronnie, who was sitting at the judges' table. She was applauding as hard as anyone. "You're the best!" Ronnie yelled.

Laurie came down from the bleachers to accept the trophy. "Thanks, everybody." She looked out over the crowd. "Just—thanks!"

As soon as Hank announced that the ceremony was over, Linda and Bob scrambled down from the bleachers to congratulate Laurie.

"Does this change how you feel about competing?" Linda asked, admiring the beautiful trophy.

"Not a chance!" Laurie said. "Today was my final competition."

"That's what I call going out in style," Bob said.

Laurie nodded. "I get to keep the trophy at home

for a year. Then it's good-bye, competing—hello, teaching." Laurie smiled at Ronnie as she joined the group.

"There's another reason I'm glad this is my final competition," she said. "With Ronnie just riding next year, I wouldn't stand a chance. Her name will be next on the trophy."

"I don't know about that," Ronnie said. "But I'll give it my best."

Maybe the year after that will be my turn, Linda thought. She blushed as she glanced up and saw Bob grinning at her. She knew he had read her thoughts.

Bronco and Doña were slowly making their way over to join them. Bronco had his camera around his neck and wanted to take pictures of the two champions—Bob with his ribbon and Linda with hers.

"One more picture," Linda said when Bronco finished and started to put the lens cover back on the camera. "Just a second." She ran over to Laurie and Ronnie and pulled on their arms. They followed her back to Bronco and Doña.

Bronco took a picture of Linda, Ronnie, and Laurie

with their arms around one another and grins on their faces.

When the pictures were over, Doña slipped her arm around Linda's waist.

"Well, dear?" she asked with a smile. "Was it as much of a challenge as the brochure said?"

Ronnie looked slightly sheepish when she heard that.

But Linda just grinned. "Doña," she said, "you wouldn't believe it."